CRIME TRAVELERS

BOOK 3

PRICELESS

An International Adventure Novel
Featuring Lucas Benes and the NEW RESISTANCE

PAUL AERTKER

FLYING SOLO PRESS

BARCELONA | ROME | SEATTLE | LONDON | NEW YORK | PARIS
DENVER | HONG KONG | CAPE TOWN | LOS ANGELES | SAN JOSE

Library Metadata
Aertker, Paul
Crime Travelers / Paul Aertker.— 1st ed.
p. 240 cm. 12.7 x 20.32 (5x8 in) — (Priceless ; bk. 3)

Summary: Lucas Benes faces his greatest challenge yet when he finds a secret message from his mother hidden inside a sunken cargo container. In a near-death scuba-diving experience, Lucas and the New Resistance kids learn that Good Company CEO Siba Günerro—along with her newest and most beautiful Curukians—is planning a massive art heist. Lucas and friends scour the Spanish countryside looking for clues. But to unravel the mysteries of both the robbery and the cryptic message, Lucas must first discover the only thing that is worth more than priceless.

This is an edge-of-your-seat adventure. Strap your children in for this wild ride in the third installment of the best-selling middle-grade travel series. If your children love excitement, don't miss this action-packed read! © 2016, FSP

1. Travel—Fiction. 2. Language and languages—Fiction.
3. Conspiracies— Fiction. 4. Trains—Fiction. 5. Bankruptcy—Fiction.
6. Geography— Fiction. 7. Multicultural—Fiction. 8. Europe—Fiction.
9. Spain—Fiction. 10. Alhambra—Fiction.
I. Title. Pro 2016
Edited by Brian Luster using the Chicago Manual of Style, 16th edition | Cover design by Pintado | Maps by Paul Devine | Interior design by Amy McKnight | All designs, maps, graphics, photographs © 2016 Paul Aertker and Flying Solo Press, LLC

ISBN-13:978-1-940137-37-7 / ISBN-10:1-940137-37-3
eISBN 978-1-940137-38-4
Priceless | Printed worldwide
US Copyright Registration Number: TX 8-412-776
Library of Congress Control Number: 2016953232

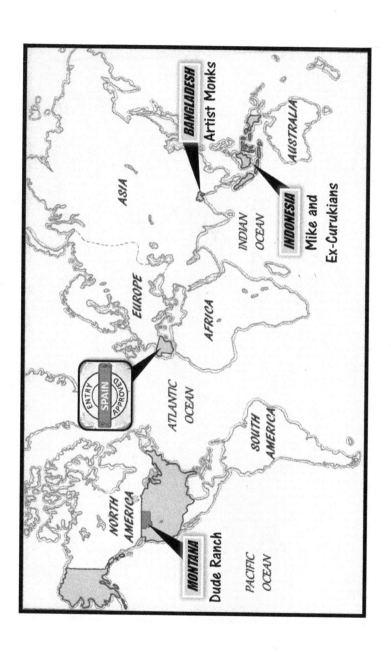

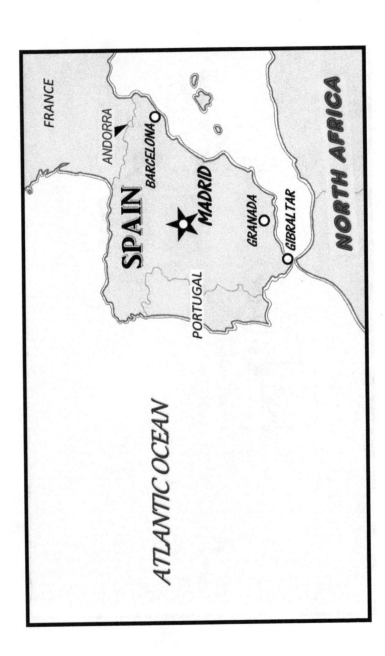

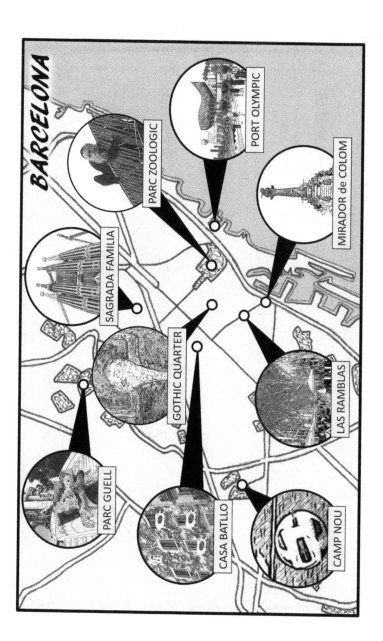

NEW RESISTANCE NOTEBOOK

SPAIN

CAPITAL
Madrid

LANGUAGE
Spanish

POPULATION
47,000,000

AREA
506,000 sq km

NOTES
Action Destination

IBERIA

COUNTRIES
Spain, Portugal,
Andorra, Gibraltar

LANGUAGES
Spanish, Portugese,
Catalan, Basque,
Galacian and others

NOTES
Home to the
endangered Iberian lynx

INDONESIA

CAPITAL
Jakarta

LANGUAGE
Indonesian

POPULATION
225,000,000

AREA
1,901,000 sq km

NOTES
Ex-Curukians from here

CATALONIA

CAPITAL
Barcelona

LANGUAGE
Catalan and Spanish

POPULATION
7,600,000

AREA
32,000 sq km

NOTES
Autonomous region of Spain

BANGLADESH

CAPITAL
Dhaka

LANGUAGE
Bengali (Official)

POPULATION
171,000,000

AREA
148,000 sq km

NOTES
Monk artists are from here

GIBRALTAR

**BRITISH OVERSEAS
TERRITORY**
Located on the SE tip of the
Iberian peninsula

POPULATION
32,000

AREA
6.7 sq km

NOTES
A big splash happens
here

MYANMAR

CAPITAL
Naypyidaw

LANGUAGE
Burmese

POPULATION
51,000,000

AREA
677,000 sq km

NOTES
Formerly known as Burma

MONTANA

A STATE IN THE USA
Borders Canada

POPULATION
1,000,000

AREA
381,000 sq km

NOTES
Lucas went to a
Dude ranch here

CONTENTS

You can travel by boat, by bike, or by book.
Yet with your imagination you can go anywhere by any
means at any time.
—P.A.

GET THE KIDS

The Globe Hotel Barcelona sat on top of a hill overlooking a harbor filled with superyachts.

It was an old stone palace that had seen better days. Vandals had tagged the walls with graffiti, some windows were missing panes of glass, and its multicolored roof had cracked and broken tiles. The main building had once been a megamansion fit for a king. Or rather, fit for a dictator, since Franco, the former Spanish ruler, liked to bring frenemies here for torture.

It was fair to say that the Globe Hotel Barcelona was far from being the luxurious residence that Mr. John Benes had wanted. His hope had always been to renovate the place and turn it into a family resort with mud baths for parents and giant water slides for kids.

In reality, many of the bathtubs were filthy, and the pool slide was ready to crumble into the water.

Except for the colonies of mice that inhabited the place, the building had remained nearly empty for a decade. The few human guests who had actually stayed at the resort had written online that a single night's stay at the hotel gave them nightmares for weeks on end.

Since the number of negative reviews had turned off most would-be visitors, it was the perfect place for Mr. Benes and Coach Creed to create another hotel spy school.

For their part, the kids of the New Resistance had been excited to spend an extended vacation in a near-abandoned palace. But when they saw the hotel for the first time, most agreed the entire property looked like a run-down roach motel.

One of the first things Mr. Benes did to improve student life was to hire a butler. But not just any old servant.

Rufus Chapman was a seventy-year-old British butler who knew what was proper and what was not. More than that, he had experience in turning derelict dumps into ritzy resorts.

On Rufus's first day at work, Mr. Benes had given him an order to pick up Lucas and his friends on the seventh floor.

The conversation had taken place down in the hotel's basement.

As usual Mr. Benes was wearing a dark suit, white shirt, and tie when he opened the swinging metal doors that led to an enormous industrial kitchen.

"Chapman," Mr. Benes said. "Do me a favor and get the kids, would you?"

Rufus was wearing an apron over his tuxedo,

complete with tails and top hat. He looked up from a giant paella pan he was stirring.

"Happy to oblige, sir," Rufus said. "Any trouble?"

"We may have some unwanted guests here at the hotel."

"Good Company?"

"Possibly."

"I would be pleased to look into the matter for you," Rufus said. "What time would you like for me to get the children?"

"Soon," Mr. Benes said. "Certainly by seven this morning. I want these kids to help put this hotel back together today because you and I will be busy with board meetings all day tomorrow."

"Tomorrow is often the busiest day of the week, sir."

"It often is."

"Not to worry," Rufus said. "We'll get this place into tip-top shape soon enough."

"I hired you for more than that," Mr. Benes said. "You know secrets about the Good Company that no one else knows."

Rufus cleared his throat. "I'll help where I can."

The two men looked at each other and paused a second.

"Sir? Should I also gather up Alister, Astrid, Kerala, Nalini, Paulo, Sora, Travis—"

"It seems you've studied the student roster, Chapman."

"Indeed," he said.

"Paulo Cabral goes by Jackknife, by the way."

Rufus Chapman nodded. "Duly noted. People tend to respond more positively when you know their names."

"No hurries, Chapman. Astrid is headed to Lucas's room now to share the news about the Good Company possibly going bankrupt."

Rufus said, "Finally! Some bad news for the Good Company."

"Coach Creed and I certainly hope you can help us in that regard," Mr. Benes said.

"Consider it done."

"Great," Mr. Benes said. "But first get the kids. And know that Lucas won't get out of bed unless a grown-up makes him."

"I have the remedy for that," Rufus said. "My morning whistle will literally shock him out of bed."

"Nevertheless, get Lucas and anyone else in his room and bring them to the main ballroom for breakfast and an all-school meeting."

"Is Dr. Kloppers cracking the whip?"

"She's still in Las Vegas, but I know she's anxious for me to get this academic year started on time."

"Very well," Rufus said. "I shall mollify any rough situation I should encounter."

"Thank you," Mr. Benes said. "I hope you're happy here."

"I'm delighted not to be working for Ms. Günerro

anymore," Rufus said. "The Good Company has a way of twisting things around, you know."

"Yes, they do," Mr. Benes said. "We're happy you've left them and joined us."

"One more thing, sir. The young man named Mac was on the roster from the trip to Rome. Is he not among us?"

"He is no longer here," Mr. Benes said. "He's staying with his aunt."

"The one and only Siba Günerro," Rufus muttered. "Very well, I'll do as you say. Get the kids is a simple task."

Mr. Benes left the kitchen, and Rufus Chapman handed a wooden spoon to one of the sous-chefs who had just come in.

Rufus hung his apron on a wooden peg. From another hook he took a silver medal that he had won at last year's International Whistling Convention and draped the ribbon over his head.

Rufus shuffled his patent leather shoes across the dusty basement floor, whistling a medley of national anthems. He cut through the overflow luggage room, around the hotel's massive furnace, and headed up the back stairs.

There was only one problem. With his head now full of music Rufus Chapman began to breathe more deeply. The constant whistling had the effect of draining his brain of oxygen, which seemed to make Rufus light-headed, a tad bit daft, from time to time.

On the landing between the first and second floors, Rufus stopped and rubbed his brow. Something was not right.

Unwanted guests here at the hotel?

Rufus whistled up the stairwell and waited for the echo. He mulled the instructions over in his head. The expression Mr. Benes had used, "get the kids," simply meant "pick them up."

To Rufus, who had grown up in London, the term had a positive meaning. His mum used to say to his dad, "Honey, would you be a buttercup and get the kids for me?" The buttercup part, he knew, was a bit cheesy. Still, the phrase had always been a well-meaning line.

He considered the opposite. *The Good Company has a way of twisting things around.*

The last time he had heard the expression "get the kids," it had come from Ms. Siba Günerro. Her definition meant "snatch the children and torture them into telling her about some secret that would make her richer."

Rufus Chapman suddenly became very worried. He knew that if the Good Company was involved, things would not be as good as they seemed.

A HOTEL OF CARDS

Lucas Benes lay under a flowery bedspread at the Globe Hotel Barcelona having a nightmare.

So many things were wrong with the world from his point of view. His mind struggled to make sense of it all.

Lucas dipped deep into a dream where he was drowning in a sea of diamonds. As his body sank to the sandy seafloor, he felt as if he were chained in a dark dungeon. He tried to scream, but no one could hear him. He swam through a forest of seaweed and found a key and he jammed it into a lock and broke free.

In the hotel bed Lucas tossed and turned, then was suddenly awakened by the sound of a big, giant fart.

"Ah," he said. "Cut it out, Jackknife."

"Don't look at me, bro," said the dark-haired Brazilian.

"Alister?" Lucas asked. "Was that you?"

"Not me, mate," said the bow-tie-wearing kid.

Lucas sat up in his bed and squinted. With one open eye he saw Nalini wearing one of her colorful Indian sarongs. She was rocking Gini, the baby, back and forth in a stroller.

Gini said, "Whoopsie."

The almost-two-year-old then proceeded to stink up her diaper and the room.

"Listen," Lucas said. "I don't want to wake up like that. Morning is for break*fast,* not break *wind.*"

Lucas sank back into his pillow. He had traveled so much in the last few months that his jet lag had almost lapped him and canceled itself out. He tried to shake off the slumber and weird dream as he ran his fingers through his bed-head hair.

A slice of sunlight cut through a crack in the curtains, highlighting a quarter of the room. The place had been decorated so long ago that it had gone out of style and back in without ever being changed. It was clean and the sheets were new, but the daisy table nestled in the corner with its plastic retro chairs had clearly been there for decades. The old tube-filled TV looked like it had a swollen butt sticking out the back.

Around him he could feel the small vibrations of the concrete building. Water rushed through pipes and an elevator dinged somewhere in the distance.

Sleep faded, and Lucas breathed deeply with one open eye traveling across the room. Travis was already gone. Jackknife lay on the other bed reading a book. Nalini was unbuckling Gini from the stroller.

In the corner a floor lamp cast a yellowed light on Alister Thanthalon Laramie Nethington IV, who was leaning over a giant house of playing cards. The kid from the Falkland Islands plopped a card into place and slowly crabbed around the back side of the table. He looked up, and his eyes connected with Lucas.

"It's a hotel of cards," Alister said.

"Hmm," Lucas mummed.

"Hey, mate," Alister said.

"Yeah."

"Some bloody bad dreams you had last night."

Lucas's eyelid closed again as he slid into the dark of his mind. The nightmare wasn't over. It was like a sickness that kept coming back again and again.

He knew he was still in Spain. Or least he thought he was.

Have we only been here three days? Lucas thought. *Not even. Just three nights?*

In his mind Lucas replayed the film from the previous week.

They were on a boat, a ship in the Mediterranean. Alister had cut a giant hole, a gash in a metal container, and Lucas had caused it to scatter diamonds across the sea floor.

There was the kid, Mac, who was Siba Günerro's nephew.

"He was a traitor," Lucas said aloud in the room.

Alister, Jackknife, and Nalini looked at Lucas like he was crazy.

Lucas sank deeper into his memory. The whole summer had been a series of tricks, ruses, and pure deceit. It had started when a boy with a scar on his neck had dropped off Gini (and her dirty diaper) in a shopping cart at the back parking lot of the Globe Hotel Las Vegas.

"No," Lucas said out loud. "That wasn't the beginning."

Lucas crawled further into his past to a time when he was a baby and Astrid's mom had put him in a Styrofoam ice chest to save him from an exploding ferryboat in Tierra del Fuego. He had wrecked the Good Company's brainwashing bus in Paris. Then, last week, brainwashed Curukian boys had thrown him off a container ship in the Mediterranean. To drown.

Everywhere I go, Lucas thought. *Water, water, everywhere.*

He snapped his head forward and sat straight up in bed, the words from his half dream spilling out of his mouth.

"We've got to do something different," Lucas yelled into the room.

Alister jumped, nearly flattening a quarter of his hotel of cards.

"Who are you talking to?"

"I was having a . . ."

"It's called a nightmare," Nalini said.

Jackknife added, "He's been like this three nights.

Talking in his sleep."

"What'd I say?"

"You kept repeating a line," Alister said.

"What?"

"You kept saying," Jackknife said, "'Might be worse.'"

"And," Alister said, "you also said, 'Might be better.'"

Lucas pressed his fingers over his eyes. "I think I meant those boys. Everything seems so terrible for them and I know that's why they're bad, but it could be better for them. For the Curukians."

"Curukians in your dreams," Nalini said. "Definitely a nightmare."

While still in bed, Lucas grabbed a pair of shorts and slipped them over his boxers. Just as he was sliding his feet into a pair of flip-flops, the door to the hallway opened.

Lucas thought it was odd that someone was using a master key without knocking first. Even Coach Creed knew to tap on the door before entering. But Lucas was mostly worried that the rush of air might tornado through Alister's hotel of cards.

Jackknife flipped from his bed to the floor and pretended to prepare for a fight.

Carrying a newspaper under her arm, Astrid burst into room 725, her blond hair trailing behind her.

"You could knock," Lucas said.

"The electronic locks on all the doors in the hotel are not working."

"I think my hotel of cards," Alister said, "might be in better shape than this place."

"Yeah," Astrid said, "the one working elevator feels like it's about to crash." She pushed past Nalini and Gini. "Wow. It stinks in here!"

"Yeah, Nalini," Alister said. "Gini's great and all. But why did you bring her up here?"

Nalini turned the stroller. "I'm babysitting, so I can't leave her," she said. "But I came up here to see if you guys had met the new person yet?"

"Good, I won't be the new kid anymore," Alister said.

"It's not a kid," Nalini said. "Lucas and Astrid's dad hired an English butler to put this place as he said, 'into tip-top shape!'"

"Did you meet him?" Astrid asked.

"I overheard him talking to your dad in in the kitchen," Nalini said. "He's wearing a tuxedo with tails and a top hat."

"Nice," Jackknife said.

Astrid crossed her arms. "Well, what about him?"

"His name is Rufus," Nalini said.

"Great name," Alister said.

"He's from London," Nalini continued, "and he has a silver medal from the International Whistling Convention."

"Wow," Jackknife said. "Always been a dream of mine: competitive whistling."

"He can supposedly whistle every national

anthem," Nalini said. "But we're supposed to wait for him to pick us up."

"Why?" Lucas asked.

Nalini said, "Mr. Benes thinks someone from the Good Company may have broken into our hotel last night."

"So?" Jackknife said. "That was last night."

Nalini said, "They might still be here."

WHISTLING CHAMPION

The combination of climbing the stairs and whistling was making Rufus Chapman woozy. When the seventy-year-old butler pushed open the door to the seventh floor, he nearly fainted. He stepped into the hallway and leaned the tails of his tuxedo against the wall. As he pushed his top hat up, he wiped his brow.

Rufus scanned the hallway. A sign on the wall pointed to rooms 701 to 725. Between rooms 703 and 704, there was a glass case housing a fire hose wrapped on a spool. Two broken sconces flickered light on the wall, and the carpet smelled of old sweat. All the doors were closed. Rufus let out a long whistle, holding it as if calling out to someone far down the corridor.

Nothing came back.

The butler glanced at his watch and saw that he had a few minutes to catch his breath.

While Rufus waited for oxygen to return to his bloodstream, he heard a curious series of groans coming from room 701. He approached and cupped his ear close, listening for the suspicious sound to come again.

Suddenly the door sprang open and startled Rufus. He stumbled back.

Standing in the doorway was Charles Magnus, head of Good Company Security. Magnus was clean-shaven and dressed exactly like Rufus in a tuxedo with tails and top hat.

"Nice monkey suit," said Magnus in a fake British accent.

"You frightened me," Rufus said. "I thought I was looking at a mirror of my younger self."

The two men laughed.

"You look terribly familiar," Rufus said, searching his foggy mind for a memory. "Do I know you from London, perchance?"

"Just another handsome face," Magnus said.

The two men chuckled.

"Room 701?" Rufus asked. "Under what name are you registered at the hotel?"

"My name?" Magnus said. "I'm Charles Sungham."

"Pleasure to meet you, Mr. Sungham," Rufus said, extending a warm handshake. "I'm Rufus Chapman, head butler here at the Globe Hotel Barcelona."

"Just the man we were looking for!" Magnus said, pointing to the back of the hotel room. "We're all in these penguin suits because we're going to a wedding."

Rufus whistled the "Wedding March" as two more men wearing tuxedos emerged from the back of the room. One was tall, and the other sported a mustache.

Both men lumbered forward and stood behind Magnus, giving Rufus a clear view into the room.

"A wedding?" Rufus asked. "I'm sorry—I don't recall seeing a wedding booked on the hotel's calendar for today."

"It's taking place down at the Sagrada Família."

"Beautiful place."

"We're having a bit of a problem," said the mustached man. "Hoping you could be of assistance."

"It's my pleasure and duty to serve," said Rufus.

The tall man standing directly behind Magnus said, "My brother back here is having trouble tying this bloody bow tie."

Rufus glanced at his watch.

"In a hurry?" Magnus asked.

"I have some children to pick up."

"At what time?" asked the mustached man.

Rufus spoke without thinking. "Seven a.m. sharp."

"What room are you picking the kids up in?" asked the tall man.

Something was not right. Through his nose, Rufus inhaled deeply as he tried to quicken the oxygen to his brain. But the forest of hair in his nostrils slowed the flow of air.

Rufus yawned. "Seven two five."

"Only twenty-four little rooms away," said the mustached man.

"Ah!" said Magnus as he closed the door behind Rufus. "You've got plenty of time."

"Should always help another when in need," said the mustached man. "Right?"

Rufus hesitated. "I presume so."

"Spoken like a true gentlemen," said a voice from the back of the room.

Rufus followed the voice and rounded the corner of the hotel room. A fourth man was sitting on the bed, trying to knot a bow tie. He had dark hair and a full beard. The man looked up at Rufus and dropped the tie to the carpet.

Then, like a bolt of lightning, he charged headfirst into Rufus's gut, sending both of them flying into the closet door.

The tall man threw open the sliding panel while Magnus ripped sheets from the beds. Rufus struggled for air as he lay on the floor of the closet.

The men piled on. The mustached man rammed a pillowcase into Rufus's mouth, gagging him, while the others spun the sheets around his arms and legs, like cowboys roping a calf.

Rufus groaned and squirmed.

The men tossed bedspreads into the closet and closed the door.

"Let's go," Magnus said.

"You said there was no hurry," said the mustached man.

"Listen," Magnus said as he stared at the men before him. "I've been trying to quit the Good Company for almost a year now."

"What?" asked the tall man.

"News flash," Magnus said. "The Good Company is going broke. I haven't been paid in nearly six months."

"Horrible," said the tall man.

"She's been paying us with five-hundred-euro notes," said the bearded man.

"They're fake," Magnus said. "Counterfeit. Probably from her frenemy in Bangladesh."

The tall man asked, "Who's that?"

"His name is Ching Ching," Magnus said. "That's all I know."

"I knew something was up with that lady," the mustached man said.

"Yeah," said the bearded man. "We should quit."

"I know *I* should," Magnus said. He paused and dropped his head. "To be honest with you, I feel terrible. I've been the quiet guy forever. I said yes to everything Siba asked for, and I never said no to all the awful things we did. I didn't want any of it. All I really wanted was a Maserati and an island."

"That's sounds sweet," said the mustached man.

"Who doesn't want that?" asked the bearded man.

"We could have made a fortune this summer," Magnus said. "A mass kidnapping in Paris and a diamond container in Rome. And each time it was botched."

The three men nodded.

"What's the one common denominator?" Magnus asked rhetorically. "It's a kid down the hall by the name of Lucas Benes." Magnus huddled his group. "We're all in this for the money, right?"

The men's heads moved up and down.

"If we are ever going to get any money from the Good Company, it will be with this next job that Günerro is thinking about. But if we get Lucas to tell us what that secret message in the sunken container means, then we'll get there first and we'll be rich forever."

"Yeah," said the bearded man.

"What happens if it doesn't work out?" asked the mustached man.

"After today," Magnus said, "either one of two things is going to happen."

"What's that?" said the mustached man.

"I can't do this anymore," Magnus said. "I'll do it one more time if I can get the secret treasure from Lucas—then I'll slip away to my island and be gone forever; otherwise, I'll have to come clean and tell the truth."

"You serious?" asked the mustached man.

"Yes," Magnus said. "I'm going to spill the beans on Siba Günerro and her Good Company—to the police."

"You'll go to jail," said the tall man.

"Negative," Magnus said. "I'll get immunity."

"What's that?" asked the bearded man.

"Basically it's protection. I tell the cops all about Ms. Günerro and her Good Company and she goes to jail and I go free."

"Either way," said the tall man, "we're with you."

"Let's do it then," said the bearded man. "For good."

He put his arm in the center of the group. The others chimed in and stacked hands like a team preparing for a game.

"For good!" they said in unison, their arms rising.

"You heard the butler," said the man on the bed. "Room 725."

"I'll use me British accent," said the mustached man.

Magnus looked at the others and smiled. "As Siba would say," he said, "get the kids."

KNOCK, KNOCK

At the beginning of every school year Lucas felt like there was a whole new list of rules. Brand-new made-up laws that someone created and everyone else had to follow. For the playground. The cafeteria. School trips. And now at this hotel-school in Barcelona, he and the others had to wait on some butler just to come pick them up. Lucas was certain this new guy would have a truckload of his own control systems. Secretly Lucas hoped there would be a ban on girls coming into his room. That would be a rule he could follow.

"Not to be rude," Lucas said, "but can you girls please get out of our room? At least let us get up first?"

"And take that diaper out of here, would you?" Jackknife said. "It stinks like, well, you know."

"We have to wait," Nalini said. "Something's going on with our hotel and the Good Company." She huffed and snatched Gini up to carry her to the bathroom. She closed the door behind her, and the diaper smell seemed to fade.

"Why do we have to wait on a *butler* to pick us up?" Jackknife asked.

"I'm sure there's a rule," Lucas said.

"Why do we have a butler anyway?" Alister asked.

"I don't know," Astrid said. "But my dad obviously hired him for a reason."

Jackknife fell back on his bed and pulled a pillow over his head.

"Okay, Astrid," he said. "Nalini came to tell us about this whistling butler. Let me guess—you came to tell us something important about . . ."

Still holding the newspaper in her hand, Astrid stood in front of the TV.

"I came to see if you guys had read the paper?" she asked.

Alister, Lucas, and Jackknife goggled each other.

Alister said, "Sorry, but I haven't got round to it just yet."

"Top of my list, I can assure you," said Jackknife. "I plan on reading it all afternoon down by the pool instead of getting on that giant slide."

"It's off-limits anyway," Astrid said. "Coach Creed said the tubes and slides were dangerous."

"I know, I know," Jackknife said. "I would never break that rule."

On the bedside table there was a bus and metro map on top of a sealed envelope that read HOMEWORK PAPERS. Lucas pushed them aside, clicked on the lamp, and sat up in bed.

"Yeah," he said. "I'm way ahead of you. I read the paper hours ago. I was even thinking about writing a blog about it and giving it to our new English teacher."

"Who's the new English teacher?" Astrid asked excitedly.

"I have no clue," Lucas said.

"Oh be quiet," Astrid said. "I know normal kids don't read the news, but I thought you might be interested in this." She unfurled the newspaper and showed them the front page.

The headline read GOOD COMPANY MARKS ONE YEAR OF LOSING MONEY.

The boys looked at one another. Lucas felt like they had missed a few days of life.

"Since you're not going to read the article," Astrid said, "I'll tell you that it essentially says that the Good Company is on the verge of bankruptcy."

"What's that mean again?" said Jackknife. "Bankruptcy is like, um . . ."

"Alister," Astrid said. "Your dad's a banker. You want to explain?"

"Sure," Alister said. "The simple definition is where a company loses a lot of money, and they basically go out of business because they can't pay their bills. They probably owe money to a lot of people. That's called debt. And they will probably have to sell everything at super cheap prices just to pay some of the people they owe."

"Serves her right," said Jackknife. "And we're the ones who helped make that happen, too."

"In part," Lucas said. "But Ms. Günerro is still a scary lady. She'll do anything to win."

Alister dropped an ace of hearts on the third floor of his hotel construction project.

"I have a bad feeling," Alister said, "that we will soon have another go at the Good Company."

"Good," Jackknife said. "I hope we do. Finish what we started."

Astrid folded the paper under her arm. "Well," she said. "Dad and Coach Creed are in a meeting right now about the Good Company going broke."

"Why?" Jackknife asked. "Why would they be in a meeting about the Good Company?"

"Because," Astrid said, "if Ms. Günerro has to get rid of something, she might sell the Good Hotels; then our Globe Hotels might get a chance to buy Good Hotels and rename them."

"That would be great," Jackknife said. "She has awesome hotels in really nice places."

"Remember her hotel in Las Vegas?" Alister asked.

"With the ocean theme?" Jackknife asked. "That was the best."

"No offense," Alister said. "It was better than this dump in the Globe Hotel chain."

Lucas shook his head. "Before Ms. Günerro sells anything, she'll do something rash."

"Yeah," Jackknife said, adding a rhyme. "To get some extra cash."

"Maybe her plan is in that sunken container," Astrid said.

"Why do you say that?" Jackknife asked.

Astrid said, "The Good Company divers keep going into the diamond container but not coming up with any diamonds."

"How do you know all this?" Lucas asked.

"The guy who cleans the pool here at this hotel, Cesar, has a boat," Astrid said. "He took some divers out yesterday."

"And they're not getting any diamonds?" Jackknife asked.

"No," Astrid said. "The site's picked clean because there's some sort of vacuum boat out there."

"So why are the Good Company divers going into the container?" Alister asked.

"Yesterday," Astrid said, "one of the divers overheard something about a message spray-painted on the inside wall of the container."

"What did it say?" Lucas asked.

"They don't know," Astrid said. "Or at least they didn't tell the boat driver."

"Why not?" Jackknife asked.

Astrid sighed. "Because there was a team of divers that wouldn't let anyone in to see it."

Jackknife said. "That's fishy."

"Always is," Lucas said, "with the Good Company."

There came a knock at the door.

"It's the butler!" Nalini yelled from the bathroom. "Come in."

Someone knocked again.

THE BREAKFAST OF CHAMPIONS

Ms. Günerro was looking out the wide windows of her penthouse apartment at the Good Hotel Barcelona when she heard the knocking at the door.

She ignored it.

Like most successful people on the planet, Siba Günerro liked to plan things in advance. Many people booked vacations months or years ahead of schedule to secure hotels and flights to far-off destinations, beaches, and foreign cities.

The Good Company was no different.

But ever since Lucas Benes found a baby in the parking lot at the Globe Hotel Las Vegas, things had gone decidedly bad for the not-so-good Good Company.

Through the western-facing window, Ms. Günerro could see tourists snaking through Park Güell. In the other direction, boats swarmed an area off the coast where scuba divers were combing the seafloor for the remaining Kapriss diamonds that had spilled a few days earlier.

This particular morning Ms. Günerro wore a long housecoat made of West Bengal silk that shimmered in the light. She pretended not to hear the knock at the door and sat at the grand piano in the corner.

She set her fingertips on the keys and resumed playing a tune she had written as a child. It was called "I Did It the Rich Way."

Listening to this music and sprawled across the beds was the remaining portion of Ms. Günerro's security team: Goper Bradus from Greenland and Ekki Ellwoode Ekki from Iceland.

Ekki was watching a video on his phone, while Goper was picking his nose. Both guards were waiting for their uniforms to be cleaned. For the last three days they had been lounging in plush white bathrobes and pink pedicure sandals.

The knock at the door turned to a rattle and startled Ms. Günerro.

The chief executive stopped playing the piano and looked up. The sound of Ekki's video escaped his earbuds and crackled into the room. Goper flicked his booger onto the carpet and stared blankly at the ceiling.

"If you truly want more responsibility," Ms. Günerro said, "then start by getting the door."

Goper sat up. The Barcelona humidity had pumped up his blond curls so that his hair was now bigger than his actual head. The pouf looked like a golden halo floating above him.

"I'm not dressed," said Goper as he shuffled across the room, his freshly painted toenails gleaming through the shag carpet.

He opened the door and found a teenager dressed

in the resort's room service uniform. A gold name tag on his coat read ANDRÉS.

"Room service," he said, handing Goper a long plastic bag of dry-cleaned suits.

Goper hung the clothes in the closet and stepped out of the way.

The dishes on the tray clinked as Andrés wheeled a metal cart into the room. He set the breakfast table with white linens, silverware, and crystal glasses. He spread out breads and muffins, carafes of orange juice and hot chocolate, and tureens filled with eggs and ham. On one of the place mats he set an enormous golden bowl of frozen green peas. Then he pulled out a chair and set a *Good Company Gazette* on the seat.

On top of the newspaper Andrés dropped an envelope that read FROM THE DESK OF CHING CHING.

The waiter then waited with his hand upturned.

"That will be all," Ms. Günerro said to Andrés as she pressed a five-hundred-euro note into his palm.

"Wow," Andrés said, staring at the money. "I've never gotten a tip this big."

Ms. Günerro turned. "You've never met anyone as wealthy as I."

Andrés tucked the big bill into his jacket, wheeled the cart out, and closed the door behind him.

Ekki's nose sniffed the air. He tossed his phone and earbuds onto the bedspread, tightened his robe around his bulging waist, and slipped his bright red toenails into pedicure sandals.

As he shuffled to the table, he said, "Your hotels are the greatest."

"I know that," Ms. Günerro said. "I should change the name to the Great Hotels."

"Agreed," Ekki said as he loaded two mini muffins into his cheeks.

Goper and Ekki ate like hogs at a trough while Ms. Günerro funneled heaps of frozen green peas into her mouth. As she smacked her lips, she slipped on a pair of cat-eye reading glasses and glanced at the newspaper. She lifted the envelope from Ching Ching.

Ms. Günerro gulped the peas down, and her stomach grumbled. Not from the food. She had butterflies every time she heard from Ching Ching. Sure, he always had extra cash. Lots of it. But if he was writing her a note, it could only mean she owed him something. Or else.

There was always an "or else" when it came to working with Ching Ching.

As she peeled back the envelope's flap, her thumb snagged on a piece of tape. Someone had already opened the letter and resealed it. She knew something was up with Magnus. And now someone was spying on her mail. The look in her eyes shifted to worry. In a few months' time the chief executive had blown a kidnapping job in Paris and lost a treasure-filled container, both of which could have saved her company.

She glanced out the window and winced,

thinking about the jewelry she could have made with the Kapriss diamonds. Part of her was surprised how quickly things had changed. Her fortune had gone from fabulously wealthy to near bankruptcy in the span of one summer.

All because of Lucas Benes.

She slid out Ching Ching's note and let the envelope drift to the floor. She read:

> *siba,*
> *I know of your troubles. i hope the west bengal silk housecoat i left for you makes you feel better. but you may have to sell everything you own.*
> *if you want to Remain president of the Good company, your payment to me and buNguu's too must now be "priceless." fortunately, U are in spain and there are plenty of priceless objects there. i have a troupe of Artists from everywhere— bangladesh, too—that "happily" stay at my castle in granada.*
> *you will comply. or Else.*
> *sincerely, ching Ching*

Ms. Günerro folded the note and glanced at an article on the back page of the newspaper.

"Ha!" she chuckled. "Very clever, Ching Ching. Very clever."

Goper asked, "Does Ching Ching know about the secret message in the container?"

"He might," Ms. Günerro said. "But he's giving us another option. You see, reading this message requires skill, which I have a lot of. Most people would be confused by his words or see this note as a threat from Ching Ching, but I'll tell you the man is brilliant."

"How so?" Goper asked.

Ms. Günerro looked up in thought. "Ching Ching has given us a fantastic plan B if the secret message in the container turns out to be a hoax, which it could, knowing the liars at the New Resistance."

"What's plan B?" Ekki muttered.

"If plan A doesn't work out," Ms. Günerro said, "we'll be going, according to this note from Ching Ching, to a museum in Madrid."

Ekki stopped chewing. "Why?"

"To steal a painting," Goper said. "Duh, why else would you go to a museum?"

"Ching Ching is also sending me artists who can make copies of priceless paintings that we can later sell," Ms. Günerro said. "Plan B will not only be fantastic but artistic!"

"And terrific!" said Goper.

"But if they're priceless . . ." Ekki said.

"Be quiet," Ms. Günerro snapped. "You fool."

"What about plan A?" Goper asked. "The secret message and treasure."

"Good question, Goper," Ms. Günerro said. "Magnus will find out what the message Lucas Benes's mother wrote in the container actually means. And we'll find the treasure—if there is one."

Goper said, "Magnus told me that Mr. Benes had hired Rufus Chapman from the Good Hotel London."

"He knows a lot of secrets," Ekki said. "And he lost one of our superyachts one time, didn't he?"

Goper added, "Rufus Chapman is ditzy. We could use him to our advantage."

"I like the way you're thinking these days, Goper," Ms. Günerro said as she pushed her chair back. "Not to worry. Magnus has probably already taken care of Mr. Chapman."

"Yeah, but," said Ekki as he wiped egg from his lip, "Lucas has messed us up twice this summer."

"I know that!" Ms. Günerro screamed. "Lucas thinks for himself."

"He doesn't follow rules," Goper said. "That's the problem."

"I follow the rules," Ekki said.

"You follow the food," Ms. Günerro said.

Ekki shrugged. "True, but this is a breakfast of champions. Who wouldn't follow this?"

"Well, if by chance Magnus fails," Ms. Günerro said, "I have new champions to take on the New Resistance."

"Who's that?" Goper asked.

"Take your clean clothes across the hall and get

dressed in your room," she said to her security guards.

With a muffin in his mouth, Ekki asked, "Where are we going?"

"I want to show you the newest and most beautiful weapon in the Good Company arsenal."

RIGHTY TIGHTY, LEFTY LOOSEY

For the third time in a row, the mustached man in a tuxedo with tails aimed a gnarled index finger at the door marked 725.

"Master Lucas," he said. "Your ride is ready."

He rattled on the door, and the sound hammered in the hotel room.

Astrid looked at the others in the room and crinkled her eyebrows. "Your ride is ready?"

She flung the door open.

"We'll be right there," she said abruptly. "We have a diaper to change."

"Blimey!" said the mustached man. "You kids are still wearing nappies?"

Nalini came out of the bathroom carrying Gini in her arms.

"As you can see," Nalini said, "we have a baby with us. And now a clean baby."

Gini aped, "Clean baby!"

The butler's nose wrinkled. "No one told me about a baby."

"It's what we do here," Astrid said. "We take care of people. Even babies."

Nalini strapped Gini in the stroller and pushed her

out into the hallway. Lucas followed and immediately noticed the wrinkles in the man's tuxedo.

"Are you the new butler?" Lucas asked.

"Indeed I am."

The mustached impostor briefly stared at Lucas and then shifted his eyes and fake-smiled. He quickly changed the subject.

"Oh my heavens," he said, staring at Lucas's head. "Do you use product in your hair to get it to look like that?"

"No," said Lucas with proud confidence. "I'm a natural bed head."

"People would pay a fortune for fringe like that," said the man.

Astrid, Jackknife, and Alister joined the others in the hallway.

"Shall we?" said the butler as they began walking down the hall. "Yes indeed. Your ride will soon be ready."

"Ride?" Astrid asked. "We're going to an all-school meeting, aren't we?"

"It's at a secret location," said the phony butler.

"Excuse me," Alister said. "Your accent doesn't sound like it's from London."

"My family's moved around a bit."

Between rooms 715 and 714 Lucas stopped.

Coach Creed always said that when a person gives you the creeps it's for a good reason: It's because he or she probably *is* a creep.

The wrinkled tuxedo, the shifty eyes and fake smile, a ride to a secret location, and now the accent. Something wasn't adding up. Lucas's sixth sense piqued.

"I was born in Argentina," Lucas said. "Could you whistle the Argentinean national anthem?"

The impostor stopped and took a step backward. "What kind of question is that?"

Astrid started whistling the American national anthem. "What song is that?"

"How *am I* supposed to know this?"

Gini tried to whistle but just ended up spitting on Nalini.

The impostor was now edging his way toward the end of the hallway. The kids continued to follow.

"Seriously," Jackknife asked, "can you even whistle?"

At about room 704 the butler snapped, "Stop asking so many blooming questions!"

"Smart people ask questions," Astrid said. "That's how they get to be so smart."

The door to room 701 opened, and Charles Magnus, still wearing a tuxedo and top hat, stepped into the hallway. The New Resistance kids froze.

Gini said, "Uh-oh."

"Seems to me," Magnus said, "that you're just trying to get under people's skin."

Also dressed in tails and top hats, the tall guy and the bearded man stepped out of the room and stood next to the mustached impostor butler.

Lucas thought they looked ridiculous.

Astrid got into her lawyer mode. "You're violating international law by trespassing on this property. You're also guilty of breaking and entering and theft of the use that hotel room, and I'm sure—"

"Be quiet," Magnus said calmly. "I'm not Ms. Günerro and I don't want to be."

The mustached butler said, "Just tell us where the treasure is."

"What treasure?" Astrid asked.

"There's a message spray-painted on the inside of Ms. Günerro's sunken diamond container," Magnus said. "The one Lucas dropped into the Mediterranean."

Astrid clumped her long blond hair behind her. "What does the message say exactly?"

Magnus's eyes scanned the group in front of him. "You all know that Lucas's birth mother sent this container around the world to keep her father's diamonds out of Ms. Günerro's hands, right?"

Everyone nodded.

Charles Magnus cleared his throat. "One of our scuba divers just reported to us that Lucas's mommy left a note on the inside of the container about a priceless treasure."

Lucas felt his muscles tense up. He stopped listening as he tried to imagine what his mother would have looked like painting that message. He desperately wanted to know what it said.

He was sick of the way things had been going. The New Resistance kids had done a lot to stop

Siba Günerro and her stupid company. But as far as he knew, the Good Company had killed his mother for the sake of making money and brainwashed and kidnapped kids from all over the world, stolen diamonds, and killed elephants for their ivory.

What kind of world is this? he thought.

At that moment he knew he would do something about the despicable way grown-ups had run this world. It became clear to him what he needed to do. When Lucas's mind came back to reality, Charles Magnus was still talking.

". . . but if you help us," Magnus was saying, "then we can prevent Ms. Günerro from getting hold of a priceless treasure. If she gets it, the New Resistance would lose everything you'd gained this summer against the Good Company."

What? Lucas thought. *Is Charles Magnus trying to get help from the New Resistance?*

Lucas could feel Astrid, Nalini, and Jackknife staring at him, waiting for him to say something. Part of Lucas wanted to help. Another side of him was skeptical.

Sitting in her stroller, Gini stuck out her tongue. "Pppp!"

Lucas spoke. "We don't know what you're talking about."

"You're lying," Magnus said.

"Not right now," Lucas said. "None of us has ever heard of a secret treasure or a message inside the container."

"That's true," said Astrid.

"Honest," Jackknife added.

"We can make this easy," Magnus said, "or difficult. Either way, you're going to tell me what that message means and where the treasure is."

"It sounds to me," Astrid said, "that you're trying to go behind Ms. Günerro's back."

"That is true," Magnus said. "I'm tired of working for someone whose middle name is Greed."

"So," Astrid continued, "you're trying to quit before the Good Company goes broke."

Magnus's head dropped.

To Lucas the man looked defeated, almost sad, like he had just lost the biggest game of his life. Part of Lucas wanted to be nice, but his practical side knew they couldn't take a chance on Magnus. Lucas looked for an escape.

"We'd love to help," Nalini said. "But I can assure you we have no information, and that's true."

Gini said, "True dat."

Lucas looked for a solution. On his left he spotted a plate-glass window of a fire hose case. Someone had scratched out the *o* in *bombero*—the Spanish word for firefighter—to make it the Catalan word *bomber.*

Then the idea hit him like a splash of cold water.

"I smell smoke," Lucas said as he winked at Alister.

"Good try," said Magnus. "Now is not the time to yell fire in a hotel."

"This is an old building," Astrid said. "Its safety

codes are—"

"We don't smell no smoke," said the bearded man. "All we smell is some rotten kids making things difficult."

Alister looked at the others and grinned.

Lucas squatted next to the stroller as Alister's briefcase came flying through the air. The case's tiny metal feet slammed into the plate glass. Shards clattered to the carpet. Lucas sprang up, ripped part of the hose down, and whirled it in the air like a lasso.

Magnus and his men stepped back.

Astrid grabbed the handle. "Righty tighty, lefty loosey," she mumbled.

The handle squeaked as she opened the faucet. The hose shook wildly as it spun from the spool. Bracing his legs as if it were a tug-of-war, Jackknife stepped in and held the nozzle with Lucas. Behind them the hose gulped and flapped up and down like a fat anaconda writhing on the carpet.

Lucas twisted the metal head, and the water shot through the air and blasted Magnus straight in the face.

The men blocked the spray with crossed arms. Their top hats exploded off their heads.

For almost a full minute Lucas and Jackknife soaked the men from their nostrils to their knees. They nailed the tall guy in the mouth and Magnus in the eyes, and they hit the impostor butler so hard in the nose that the fake mustache sailed off his face.

From her stroller Gini let out a huge cackling giggle. The men stumbled through the doorway of their room, where they collapsed on one another like a pile of wet rags.

Astrid killed the water, and Lucas tied the fire hose around the door handle and knotted it to a door across the hall.

"If my mother left me a message before she died," Lucas said, "then I want to read it myself."

A CALL TO FINS

The kids split and left Magnus and his men trapped in room 701.

Nalini took Gini in the stroller down the elevator while Jackknife, Lucas, Alister, and Astrid bolted down the back stairs to the deck area.

On the left a giant maze of slides and tubes bridged an Olympic-sized swimming pool. At the far end a man was skimming trash from the water with a net.

"Before we do anything," Jackknife said, "let's go on the slide first."

"Here's an idea," Astrid said. "Let's use our brains first."

"I thought we were going to read this secret note from Lucas's mom?" Alister asked.

"We are," Astrid said, "but the message is inside the container that is at the bottom of the Mediterranean Sea!"

Jackknife said with a smile, "We better get our wet suits on then."

"This, my friends," Lucas said, "is an official Call to Fins."

"I like the way that sounds," Jackknife said.

Lucas nodded confidently. "Let's go find out what

that message in the sunken container really says."

Wearing gym shorts, a T-shirt with a bull on it, and flip-flops, Coach Creed emerged from the cabana dressing room. The Texan folded his beefy arms, blocking the children's forward motion.

"Hold your horses," Coach said.

"Neigh," Jackknife said.

"Where exactly do you think you're going?" Coach asked.

"We're going to the bathroom," Jackknife said. "That squid we ate last night gave us diarrhea."

"Diarrhea my eye," Coach said. "You're lying."

"We want to go down those slides and tubes," Jackknife said.

"It's closed," Coach said. "Look at it. That piece of junk is ready to fall into the pool. It's rusted and dangerous. It's off-limits for everyone. Now, tell me the real reason you're down here."

"Apparently," Astrid said, "Lucas's birth mother left a message on the inside of Ms. Günerro's sunken diamond container."

Coach's eyes widened. "What's the message say?"

"Something about," Alister said, "a priceless treasure. We think."

"We don't know exactly," Lucas said clarifying. "But we want to go find out."

Coach's eyebrows crinkled. "Where did you learn all this?"

"From Magnus," Lucas said.

"Charles Magnus?" Coach asked. "Head of Good Company Security? Where did you see him?"

Astrid pursed her lips. "He and his goons dressed up as fake butlers and broke into room 701, and they were trying to get us to tell them about this secret message."

"Wait a minute," Coach said. "Did our new butler, Rufus Chapman, not come up to your room?"

"No," Lucas said. "We never met him."

Coach asked, "So where's Magnus now?"

"Lucas and Jackknife blasted them with a fire hose," Astrid said, "and then locked them in 701."

Coach Creed shook his head. "What is Ms. Günerro up to now?"

"It's not her," Astrid explained. "Magnus is trying to break away from Ms. Günerro, and he's trying to get to this treasure before she does. He's quitting the Good Company."

"That doesn't surprise me," Coach said. "A lot of grown-ups end up hating their jobs."

"What do you think?" Lucas asked. "Is there really some priceless treasure?"

"First off, I don't know about this message," Coach said. "And secondly, you've got to dig deep on that question of priceless." He paused to make sure the kids were listening. "Priceless is subjective, meaning it's from your point of view. We have to figure out what was priceless to your mother, or more importantly what she thought it would mean to you."

No one said anything. Lucas had a sense of what he thought priceless might be, but he couldn't quite put his finger on it.

From the side of the hotel, Travis Chase banked a skateboard around the pool man, who was now pushing a trash cart. The Californian rolled past the giant water slide and up to the group. He popped his board up into his hand.

"Looks like you guys are going someplace," he said. "Whatever it is, I'm in."

"Hey, Coach," Jackknife asked. "Can we ask the pool guy if he can take us scuba diving? What's his name?"

"Cesar Vantes," said Astrid.

"Coach?" Lucas asked. "Can we?"

Overhead a dozen birds squawked loudly. They were black-and-white magpies that stormed in and landed in the grass by the pool. The birds hopped around in a circle, fighting over a chunk of bread. Suddenly the brawl broke up, and they took off over the hotel and into the blue sky.

Coach Creed looked around. "I need to deal with Magnus and his men first, and I have to find out what happened to Rufus Chapman."

Lucas stood straight and loaded up his arguments. "If we don't find that treasure first, then Ms. Günerro will."

"I know," Coach said. "And the Good Company will be right back on top." He put his hands on his head and sighed. "Dr. Kloppers is going to be furious about not starting school."

"That's okay by me," Jackknife said.

"Dr. Kloppers is still in Las Vegas," Lucas said. "She'll never know."

"Exploration," Travis said, "is a form of learning."

"I just don't want to send you out alone," Coach said.

Astrid argued for the group. "Each one of us has more than a hundred dives logged in our books, and Travis is one test away from being a master diver. This would be our education today."

"Please," Jackknife begged. "I mean, what could go wrong?"

Coach breathed deeply. "Can I trust you kids to go straight to the dive site and return immediately?"

"Yes, sir," they said in unison.

"We'll be back before lunch," Astrid said. "It's a forty-five-minute dive, at most."

Coach pointed toward the man cleaning the pool. "Okay. Cesar can take you in his boat. He knows exactly where the container is."

"Great," Travis said. "We'll get ready."

"What about breakfast?" Jackknife asked. "I'm hungry."

"Cesar should have some food in the scuba van," Coach said. "Get your suits on and get out of here. Quick."

THE NEWEST WEAPON

A crowd had gathered outside the Good Hotel Barcelona. Speaking English to a group of tourists, a young guide pointed out the odd-shaped buildings around the square that were designed by the famous architect Gaudí. She stopped speaking, and everyone turned toward the front doors of the hotel.

Siba Günerro was wearing a luxurious ivory-colored silk dress that shimmered in the midmorning light. Her high heels clomped down the marble steps, and the tourists moved out of her way.

Walking a half step behind their boss, Ekki and Goper were wearing green shorts, short-sleeve security shirts, and high-top tennis shoes.

At the top step, Andrés stopped them. "Your uniforms look great."

"They do," Goper said, "Thank you for cleaning them and delivering them to us."

"Where are you guys going?" Andrés asked.

"It's a secret," Goper said, as he put an earbud into one ear.

"If this secret doesn't work out," Ekki whispered to Andrés, "we're going to a museum in Madrid."

Goper and Ekki followed Ms. Günerro as they

descended the stairs. Ekki took the other earbud, and the two men danced as they trailed Ms. Günerro down the steps and through the streets of Barcelona.

Ms. Günerro strolled across a plaza and up a wide avenue as if she owned the city, the guards boogying behind her. They cut diagonally across the famous Eixample neighborhood filled with elegant restaurants and expensive shops.

In about fifteen minutes they arrived at the Casa Batlló with its colorful walls and balconies that resembled theater masks.

Ekki and Goper gawked at the apartment building that looked like it had come from another planet.

Tourists gathered outside taking pictures.

Next to the metro stop and across the walking path, a dozen girls sat on twelve mopeds.

In their matching yellow rompers, they resembled schoolgirls in uniform. But their long hair, white on one side and black on the other, gave them an evil, skunklike look.

Ms. Günerro flicked her wrist, and in seconds the girls lined up in front of her and stood at attention.

"These girls," Ms. Günerro said to Ekki and Goper, "are the newest weapon in the Good Company arsenal."

"But," Ekki said, "they're girls."

"No duh," Goper said.

"But girl Curukians?" Ekki asked.

"Yes," Ms. Günerro said. "I think girls are smarter

than boys."

Goper asked, "Isn't it that people are judged more on the content of their thinking . . ."

"Yeah," Ekki said, scratching his head. "I was thinking that too."

Ms. Günerro shook her head at Ekki.

Goper tried to change the subject. "What about Mike Mar?"

"Mike?" Ms. Günerro asked.

"The Burmese kid with the scar on his neck," Goper said. "He's a boy and a smart Curukian too."

"Burma is now called Myanmar," Ms. Günerro said. "My friends overthrew the government there in a coup, and we—I mean, *they*—changed the name of the country."

"Oh," Ekki said.

"Myanmar," Ms. Günerro said. "I like things that start with me or my or I." She paused a second. "So anywho . . . Mike Mar from Myanmar. I just sent him on an errand, but I didn't know his name. We must have changed it for him. To answer your question, Goper: Yes, he's been well trained."

"How do you know for sure?" Ekki asked.

Ms. Günerro cut her eyes toward Ekki. "The scar on Mike's neck came from when Ms. T drove a motorboat over his head. The kid was snorkeling in the Andaman Sea just off the coast from our school there. Nearly frightened the little devil to death."

She chuckled.

"Speaking of the—Ms. T," Goper asked with a stutter. "Where is she exactly?"

Ms. Günerro said. "Ms. T has been busy training these new *terrific* Curukian girls."

"So the *T* in her name doesn't mean *torture*?" Goper asked. "It really means *terrific*?"

"Yes, more points for you, Goper," Ms. Günerro said. "Ms. T is terrific, and as you can see from these fine girls, Ms. T's name also stands for Top Teacher."

"Some teachers," Ekki said, "are terrible."

Goper shook his head.

"Good, good, good," Ms. Günerro said. "I'm glad you like Ms. T, because she's in the hotel basement setting up shop."

"Why?" Ekki asked.

"In case," said Ms. Günerro. "In case Lucas Benes and his friends need some teaching of some kind."

"Oh," Ekki said, knocking himself on the head. "That's right! She's a teacher. I get it now. I get it. Teachers teach."

"Be quiet," Ms. Günerro said. "Just close your mouth. Would you?"

"Oh, yes."

Ms. Günerro turned and looked directly at the girl in the middle, whose hair was 100 percent powder white. On her right cheek she had a black mole.

"Bleach," Ms. Günerro said to the girl.

"Yes?" Bleach said, standing a little taller.

"Goper is smart," Ms. Günerro said, "wise, even,

to bring up this boy with the scar, Mike Mar. Do you know him?"

"We trained together at the Good Trade School in Bangladesh," Bleach said. "He's very crafty. I don't trust him."

"Don't worry about him," Ms. Günerro said. "In the end Mike is trustworthy. He'll do anything I ask, and more importantly, he'll double-cross Lucas and the New Resistance."

"Yes," Bleach said. "I understand."

"I don't want to take any chances right now," Ms. Günerro said. "You know about the sunken container?"

"Yes, I do," Bleach said.

Ms. Günerro leaned forward and looked Bleach directly in the eyes. "I want you to take a team to the dive site. My guess is that you'll be lucky and Lucas Benes will show up. If he does, I want you to find out if he knows anything about this secret message from his mother. If he doesn't . . . well then, accidents do happen."

"Accidents don't happen," Bleach said. "They are caused."

Ms. Günerro glanced at Ekki. "You see, that is why these girls are smart."

"Get your scuba gear," Ms. Günerro said to the girls. "It's time for you to get your feet wet and put Ms. T's training to good use."

I'M WATCHING YOU

Dressed in swimsuits decorated with the flags of their countries, Lucas, Astrid, Travis, and Alister came out of the dressing rooms, ready to go diving.

Robbie Stafford was a fifth-year senior from Australia who was essentially head boy of the New Resistance. The eighteen-year-old was wearing a tan poplin suit with a red tie, and he and a group of New Resistance kids had gathered outside the waiting scuba van.

Robbie approached Lucas. "Here," he said, handing over a white plastic pad. "Take this."

"What's this?" Lucas asked.

"It's a wrist slate," Robbie said.

"What's it for?"

"Writing notes underwater."

"Cool," Jackknife said, looking over Lucas's shoulder.

Robbie handed Travis a camera, and he spoke to the group like a school principal sending kids on a tour.

"Your instructions are to dive to the container, take a few pictures of this supposed secret message, and come right back. There is no treasure hunt. After you return, we'll make plans based on what you learn. Is that clear?"

They all nodded.

From the side of the hotel, Nalini came through a pair of glass doors, wearing sandals and a colorful sarong over her Indian-flag swimsuit. She was still pushing Gini in the stroller.

Kerala followed wearing no makeup and a black sundress over her black swimsuit.

"Wait for us!" Nalini called out.

Robbie shook his head. "Nalini, you're not taking a baby on a dive."

"It's no wonder you're in charge," Nalini said as she handed Gini over to Robbie. "You're such a doll. Thanks for taking care of her. Cheers!"

Tier One—Lucas, Astrid, Jackknife, Travis, Kerala, Nalini—and Alister climbed into the back of the old van. In their flag swimsuits, they looked like Olympians preparing for a race.

Terry Hines stuck his buzz-cut head through the group of waiting New Resistance kids.

"I want to go too," he said.

"No," Robbie said. "You're not Tier One."

"Alister's not Tier One either," Terry argued.

"Alister can pick locks," Astrid said. "And he speaks Catalan like Cesar."

"How did you know Cesar spoke Catalan?" Lucas asked.

"It was in our homework papers that Dad left in

our rooms, which I'm sure you didn't read."

Lucas thought about giving an excuse, but he knew it would only make him look even dumber.

"Terry," Robbie said, "you cause too many problems. Every time you go on a mission something goes wrong."

"That was a long time ago," Terry said.

Lucas leaned on the van's door. "Let him come along," he said. "Terry can help Cesar with the equipment in the boat."

The others in the van nodded in agreement.

Robbie adjusted Gini on his hip. "Okay," he said to Terry. "But you don't get in the water. Understood?"

Terry saluted. "Aye, aye, sir."

Gini poked Robbie in the eye. "Eye," she said.

The van started with a loud clatter and Terry closed the doors.

The inside of the van was a mess, with tools and scuba equipment scattered everywhere. Lucas moved to sit up front, but the passenger seat had stacks of books and manuals so tall that they had been strapped in with the seat belt. He plopped down behind the passenger seat on an empty air tank. A few scuba regulator hoses dangled from the ceiling.

Cesar Vantes wore a white shirt and shorts with sandals, and a seashell necklace and bracelet. With his wrist flapped over the steering wheel, he craned his head into the back of the van. Tufts of blond hair stuck out of a knitted ski cap, and a smile stretched behind a scruffy beard.

"Ready?" he said in Catalan.

"Yes," Alister answered in Catalan. "You know where to go?"

"No worries. I speak your language too," Cesar said in English with an accent. "Let's go to the beach!"

All the kids yelled in Spanish, *"¡Vamos a la playa!"*

Cesar put a cassette tape into the stereo and dropped the van into gear.

Tier One got ready. The kids tried on masks and fins and wet suits, tossing them around the back of the van.

"So, Alister," Travis asked. "Why do you speak Catalan?"

"I'm Scottish," he said. "Some Scots, like myself, think we should break away from the United Kingdom. Likewise, some people want Catalonia to be free from Spain. So it's a hobby of mine to learn the languages of countries that want to be independent."

"Thanks for the history lesson, guys," Jackknife said. "But there's some food in here that I'd like to make . . . um . . . history."

Behind the driver's seat there was a long, glass refrigerator sitting on the floor. The fridge was full of little pans of food—red peppers, garlic shrimp, squid-ink black rice, octopus, calamari, and little potato bombas.

Not exactly breakfast food, Lucas thought, *but when you're hungry . . .*

Alister leaned between the two seats and spoke Catalan. "Coach Creed said we could eat this food. Is that okay?"

"It's for the hotel restaurant," Cesar said, "but we don't have many guests. You can have it."

Alister translated by giving a thumbs-up.

The kids dove into the food. Lucas stabbed a forkful of shrimp and scooted between the two front seats.

As he peered out of the van, Lucas could feel he wasn't quite ready to go on another mission. Part of him wanted to just stay at home, at the hotel, and sleep or just veg in front a game or a TV.

Another part of him was curious and suspicious about this message that his mother had supposedly left inside the container.

Why didn't I look inside the container when we were on the ship? he thought. *Is this a Good Company trap?*

Lucas spotted his reflection in the rearview mirror. His hazel eyes widened. He checked the side-view mirrors, and his internal GPS booted up. If he was going to be successful, he would have to focus. Lucas Benes began to move beyond seeing what was in front of him and began observing everything.

The van followed cars and bikes and mopeds as they motored down the cobblestone streets and deeper into the old quarter.

"Camp Nou over there," Cesar said in accented English. "We take a detour because Real Madrid is playing Barcelona today."

With a mouth full of black rice, Jackknife called out, "You mean today's match is El Clásico?"

"Exact," Cesar said, as he turned the van away from the stadium and headed east through town.

"We should go!" Jackknife said, but no one paid him any attention.

The kids ate, and Lucas, Travis, and Jackknife leaned into the front of the van. They motored past apartment buildings, shoe shops, and pharmacies. The side streets splintered into a maze of tiny neighborhoods.

Cesar slowed as they came to a traffic circle where cars zipped around the Plaça d'Espanya.

On the other side of the Plaza of Spain stood a giant round building.

"Oh look!" Travis said. "That's a bullfighting ring!"

"It is a shopping mall now," Cesar said. "Bullfighting is banned in Barcelona."

"That's better," Nalini said, testing a scuba mask.

"What?" asked Travis. "The mall or the bullring?"

"No," Nalini said. "The ban on bullfighting is more humane."

"Why?" Jackknife said. "I think bullfighting sounds awesome."

"To kill animals for the fun of it?" Nalini said. "I'm sure it's not awesome for the animals."

This conversation ended quickly as two windowless minibuses eased up on both sides of Cesar's van. Small satellite dishes shaped like a human eyeball and an ear spun on the top of each bus. In Spanish, English, and Catalan the tagline said exactly what they didn't want to see:

GOOD COMPANY IMAGES
WATCHING AND LISTENING
SO YOU DON'T HAVE TO

"Good Company," Travis said. "Three o'clock."

"There's another one on your left," Astrid added.

"Ten o'clock," Nalini said.

In the middle of the traffic circle, Cesar jammed on the brakes. The kids rocked forward. Cars screeched to a halt. The two Good Company buses swerved but kept going. Cesar punched it, cut in front of the traffic, and burrowed the van through an underpass.

In a few minutes they came to the Mirador, the famous monument for Christopher Columbus and his first voyage to America.

Packs of tourists poured out of tour buses and down the tree-lined street of La Rambla.

Just beyond the palm trees and under a cloudless blue sky were the beaches and the Mediterranean Sea.

Within minutes they came to one of Barcelona's weird-shaped modern buildings at the Olympic village.

Wearing shorty wet suits, the kids crawled out of the van. Nalini stuffed their T-shirts and running shoes into two plastic crates and closed the doors.

Sunbathers, families under parasols, joggers, and tourists packed the beach. Some people were swimming. Boys on Jet Skis buzzed back and forth, and a few parasails floated overhead.

The New Resistance kids unloaded the scuba gear and schlepped it across the sand to Cesar's waiting boat.

The nerves in Lucas's spine tingled. For him, the group's silence felt strangely uncomfortable, almost creepy. And it felt like someone was watching them.

DIVER DOWN

The kids finished loading the wooden fishing boat with scuba gear. They climbed in, and Cesar sat at the back by the outboard motor. Terry cast off the lines, pushed the boat from the dock, hopped in, and neatly coiled the ropes around the cleats.

Cesar took off his knit hat, shook out his hair, and slipped on a pair of sunglasses. Then he spun the boat around and motored them out through the harbor, past sailboats, and around the superyachts.

Jackknife stared at one with a blue hull. "That would be my dream boat," he said as they came close to the stern of the yacht named *Omega*.

"That," Nalini said, "is an enormous boat."

"How big do you think that is?" Kerala asked.

"About eighty meters," Lucas said.

"Two hundred and sixty feet," Travis translated. "More or less."

"Look," Terry said, pointing at a sign draped over the railing. "It's for sale."

"Oh yes," Jackknife said. "We should buy it."

Everyone laughed, even Cesar.

"I wonder how much it costs?" Astrid asked.

"You have to be super rich," Alister said, "to buy a superyacht."

"Not true," Cesar said in English. "They don't have to be rich. When someone buys something expensive, all you know is that they spent a lot of money."

Cesar spun the boat past a rock jetty and into the Mediterranean Sea where the waves rolled in a calm and slow motion.

Terry Hines moved around the boat. He was clearly making a point to do the best he could.

It was midmorning, and the sun was already blazing hot. Terry mounted a tarp over their heads to keep the sun at bay. Then he set everyone up with their scuba gear. He toted tanks, defogged masks, and even breathed into each tank's octo emergency-breathing tube to make sure it was working.

When the kids had their gear, Terry held up an odd-looking scuba vest with two tanks.

He shrugged. "No one wants to use this rebreather?" he asked.

"We don't need it," said Nalini.

"It's overkill," Jackknife said.

"Put that thing up, Terry," Astrid said as she adjusted her mask.

"Rebreather regulators," Terry said, "recycle your air. It's good for the environment."

"It's too expensive to use," Cesar added. "It's not worth it."

"And Robbie already told you," Travis said. "You're

not supposed to go diving with us today."

Terry dropped his head. "I know."

Alister said, "You only need a rebreather tank if you don't want to make bubbles."

"It doesn't matter if we make bubbles," Kerala said. "This is not a long dive."

Lucas didn't say anything during this exchange. He stared out over the horizon. He was tired and trying not to look at the sea in which he had almost drowned a few days earlier.

In less than half an hour Cesar slowed the boat as they approached the dive site.

A thin slick of oil covered the surface of the water. A few diver-down buoys teetered on the waves, their flags flapping in the wind. A hundred meters away a boat with cables and hoses draped over the sides rocked back and forth.

"That's weird," Travis said.

"What?" Terry asked.

"We were talking earlier," Travis said, "about how many people were out here looking for the Kapriss diamonds."

"Maybe they got them all," Terry said.

"Possible," Travis said, pointing at the boat just in the distance. "That trawler over there is using a vacuum."

"What for?" Kerala asked.

"I guess," Travis said, "to vacuum up any diamonds off the seafloor."

"But why have diver-down flags and no dive boats waiting?" Astrid asked.

"This oil on the water," Cesar said, "tells me that several boats just left here."

"Without their flags?" Lucas asked.

"Maybe," Nalini said.

Lucas looked down through the dark water to see if he could make something out. It was just deep enough not to see the bottom.

Dark water.

Lucas knew he had to face his fears. It was the only way to overcome them. But he wasn't quite ready to tackle his greatest fear. Not yet. Not this quickly.

Jackknife fixed his fins and lowered his mask. "If we're going to do this," he said, "then let's do this."

The Brazilian held his mask to his face and took a giant step off the back deck. He splashed into the water and immediately filled his BC, his buoyancy control vest, with air.

"Travis has the GPS," Cesar said. "He leads."

Cesar put a straw hat on his head and leaned back on the motor.

"Terry and I will stay with the boat," he said. "Okay?"

One by one the kids dropped into the water. Travis and Lucas stepped off the back while Astrid, Nalini, and Alister flipped backward off the sides of the boat.

As soon as the water gripped his wet suit, Lucas felt better. The sea was calm and warm, and he would soon read a message from his mother.

CHAPTER TEN

Travis gave the okay sign and they all returned the signal. He dove, and they followed him below the surface. Behind them air bubbles rose as the kids vanished into the dark.

Diver down.

MESSAGE IN A CONTAINER

Underwater it was brunch time. At least for the fish.

Animals of all kinds swam out of the way of the New Resistance kids. A small school of spiny dogfish split in half, and a gray monk seal looked at the group and then darted into the distance.

The kids kicked their fins and dove deeper. The water turned cooler and darker.

For a moment it seemed they were moving through pure silence. Lucas looked at his friends. The expressions on their faces were tense and guarded.

Something was here. He could feel it, and he knew his friends could too.

A few meters deeper Lucas saw the sunken container. It was set sideways at an angle, with one edge jammed deep into the seafloor. Nearby a new fishing boat lay half-buried in the sand.

As the kids approached the container's doorway, they adjusted their BC vests and floated at neutral buoyancy.

Lucas cleared some water from his mask. His eyes scanned the area.

Discovery was often made by observing one's surroundings, but sometimes a person could understand a situation better by looking at what was *not* there.

Lucas immediately noticed what was missing.

The fact that there had been diver-down flags on the surface, a sunken boat, and no one at the container bothered him.

Lucas glanced over his tank. His feeling of being watched hadn't gone away. He twisted his wrist and scribbled on the underwater notepad. *Where divers?* he wrote, and showed it to the others.

They fluttered their fins and shrugged their shoulders.

Alister pointed at the giant gash he had cut in the container while they had been on the ship. The jagged slice was almost big enough for them to fit through.

Travis shook his head and signaled for the others to follow. The locks on the doors had been sliced off, but the doors were closed. Jackknife wrenched one open and let it swing to the side, and the sound gonged into the waves. The New Resistance kids flicked on their wrist flashlights and swam into the container.

Inside there was nothing. Sand from the seafloor had swept into the container and covered the bottom. Most everything had been taken out or vacuumed up except for a few broken pieces of wood left over from the crates that had held the ivory tusks. Scavengers had picked the place clean.

Lucas was there not to find diamonds or ivory or gold coins. He was there to read a message from his mother, his late mother.

There on the wall, spray-painted in bright red, was not one message, but two.

The kids floated and read:

My son will be named Lucas after Édouard Lucas the mathematician.

I thought my name meant "light," Lucas thought.

The second message read:

There are treasures far more valuable than priceless. Luz

Lucas and the others floated in the water and stared at the cryptic message for what seemed like a very long time. A cold stream of water seeped into Lucas's wet suit, sending shivers down his neck. He shook it off and racked his brain looking for a solution.

Nothing is more valuable than priceless, he thought. *It's a riddle.*

Travis snapped a couple of pictures, and the flashes filled the container, blinding them for just a second.

The nerves in Lucas's spine tingled again. He quivered and suddenly knew it wasn't just cold water nor was it just a *feeling* that someone was watching.

He *knew* someone was watching them. He tried to look through the gash, but it ran into the sandy floor and he couldn't see very far.

Lucas fluttered his fins and spun his head toward the container's doorway. A diver with a black-tinted mask was floating there using a rebreather regulator, making no air bubbles.

Then six scuba divers also using recycled-air regulators charged through the opening.

Lucas knew who they were.

The Curukians moved like spears slicing through water, their fins creating trailing currents behind them. Six black masks zeroed in on the New Resistance kids as the divers charged with shiny knives leading the way.

They came so quickly that Lucas had no time to pull his own knife from his calf sheath.

He spun to alert his friends, but they had already seen the divers coming at them. Flashlights crisscrossed the metal cave. From the corner of his mask Lucas spotted a light shining on a metal blade as it cut through the water and suddenly sliced Nalini's air hose.

Oxygen burst from the tube, engulfing Nalini in a giant cloud of tiny bubbles. She signaled Travis, who yanked the octo from his vest and gave it to Nalini. Travis kicked his fins into two of the divers' faces and knocked their masks loose as he and Nalini bolted from the container.

Flashlights and knives jabbed at each other like swords.

Astrid and one of the divers locked arms and rolled

in an endless somersault across the container until they slammed into the wall.

Lucas and Jackknife teamed up. They grabbed one of the diver's wrists and tried to wrestle the knife away. Jackknife tried to kick the divers' masks off, but these Curukians proved to be well practiced at fighting underwater. Jackknife and Lucas sank deeper into the container as the two divers backed them into the dark corner.

There was another explosion of air.

Lucas and Jackknife rolled away from the divers they were fighting.

Jackknife's hose burst into plumes of bubbles as a knife split it in two. Kerala gave him her octo, and they, too, sped toward the doorway. Kerala slapped two divers and knocked their knives loose.

During the ruckus, Alister had crawled to the bottom of the container to try to slip out unseen through the gash. But it wasn't big enough. A Curukian swooped in and stepped on him, ramming a fin into his neck. Then the diver turned off Alister's air tank.

As Lucas bolted to help, a gloved hand clawed his throat and jolted him backward.

Lucas jammed the diver's head down and leap-frogged over him. He grabbed Alister by the collar, opened his air valve, and pushed him toward the doorway.

Lucas saw that he and Astrid were the only ones left. Hovering over them like a flock of stingrays were the six divers. It was then that Lucas noticed all six were girls.

The Curukians dropped in close, and one of the divers grabbed Lucas's wrist while another girl grabbed Astrid's regulator hose and put a knife up to it.

The diver wrote on Lucas's notepad. *Priceless treasure where?*

Lucas shrugged that he didn't know.

The girl took the notepad and showed it to Astrid while another Curukian cut Lucas's regulator hose in half. Oxygen exploded from the tube as the tank released its air. Lucas spat out his regulator and breathed in as many bubbles as possible. He would have maybe two minutes to remain conscious, three minutes to live.

The cloud of oxygen around Lucas's head faded, and he could see Astrid trying to give him her extra octo. One of the girls knocked it away. Another diver put the notepad in Astrid's face. She shook her head, and the Curukian sliced her air hose. Astrid gulped the remaining bubbles.

Lucas tried to flee, but a girl kicked him to the sandy floor. He needed air. He needed his mother. He looked up at her message. The answer to the riddle was on the tip of his tongue.

The Curukian girls swam over their heads and out of the container. They closed the door behind them and locked it, leaving Lucas and Astrid to drown.

THE MOST IMPORTANT THINGS

Like robotic eels, two air hoses snaked through the gash in the sunken shipping container.

Holding what could be the last breath of her life, Astrid swam to the door and desperately tried to wedge it open.

For his part Lucas tried tunneling under the sandy floor, digging like a dog. Out of the corner of his eye he spotted the thin black tubes. At first they startled him. Lucas flinched, thinking they were sea snakes of some kind.

A fraction of a second later he reached out, grabbed the regulator, and rammed it into his mouth. He inhaled the biggest breath he had ever taken. While he filled his lungs with oxygen, he banged on the metal wall. Astrid spun around toward the noise and swam. Lucas extended the hose to her, and Astrid bit at the mouthpiece, pressing it to her lips.

For a full three minutes the two kids just floated and breathed.

Lucas didn't know who had put the hoses in through the hole, but it didn't matter. For the time being, staying alive was his only concern.

On the other side of the container Alister picked

the lock and opened the door, and he and Kerala swam back inside.

Kerala checked in with Astrid and Lucas to see if they were all right. They gave the signal that they were okay. Kerala handed her extra octo regulator to Astrid, who dropped the one coming out of the wall, took Kerala's, and began breathing normally, the bubbles flowing. Alister gave his octo to Lucas.

The two pairs swam side by side out through the open doorway. Floating near the gash in the container they spotted another scuba diver.

Terry Hines was using the rebreather and making no air bubbles. He pulled the two extra breathing regulators through the opening and reattached them to his BC vest. He joined Lucas, Alister, Kerala, and Astrid as they made their ascent.

After a fifteen-minute safety stop they popped up on the surface only to find that Cesar's boat was missing.

Lucas counted heads. Friends were the most important things in life. Deep down that's what Lucas really cared about.

Lucas called the roll in his mind. They were all there floating in their BC vests in a circle. Kerala, Nalini, Astrid, Jackknife, Travis, Alister, and Terry. In the middle of them, wearing a life jacket, Cesar bobbed up and down.

"What happened to the boat?" Kerala asked.

"The diver girls took it," Cesar said. "They are the

same girls from yesterday who were blocking the container."

"That was so scary," Nalini said. "Curukian girls? They scared me to death."

"Hey, Terry," Astrid said. "Thanks for breaking the rules and bringing that rebreather to us."

"You're welcome."

"You saved our lives," Lucas said. "Thanks."

"Make sure you tell Robbie and Sophia," Terry said. "They think I mess up everything."

"I will," said Lucas.

A humming noise filled the air, and Lucas looked up squinting. A twin-engine airplane buzzed overhead. The sounds rose and fell away. Jackknife waved for a rescue.

"So what are we going to do now?" Alister asked.

Jackknife said, "We'll have to swim."

"We're miles away!" Alister said.

"Your eyes," Lucas said to no one in particular, "are about twenty centimeters, or eight inches, off the water. If you can see the horizon, that would mean we're about one and a half kilometers, or one mile, away."

"But," Travis said, "we can't see it."

"The metric formula for the distance to the horizon is the square root of the height above the water divided by 6.752."

No one seemed to be following Lucas's math.

"So what does that mean?" Astrid asked. "We're not

exactly in math class right now."

Lucas kicked his fins and lifted his body halfway out of the water.

"I can see the beach," he said, calculating. "So that's about three kilometers away. It's less than two miles."

"To swim?" Alister said.

"We have fins and BCs filled with air," Jackknife said. "We can do this."

"Not Cesar," Nalini said. "He's only got a life jacket, no fins."

"We'll share," said Kerala.

A second later, Cesar and the New Resistance kids began the long, slow game of kick, paddle, paddle back to the shore.

After a while of swimming another buzzing sound drifted in the air. Lucas stopped and looked up, thinking it was another plane. The noise skipped across the surface of the water as nine Jet Skis came into view.

"They're back," Nalini said. "I don't like these Curukian girls."

"Let's get underwater," Jackknife said.

"We can share air," Astrid said. "Quick."

Lucas flutter-kicked again and rose up.

"Wait," he said. "They're not girls."

Within thirty seconds the Jet Skis had encircled them.

All nine were shirtless Curukians wearing black cut-off jeans.

"Lucas," said the boy in the center. "Do you remember me?"

The motors rumbled as the Jet Skis rocked in the water, and the air smelled of fuel.

Lucas saw the scar on the boy's neck. He was the kid who'd dropped Gini off in the back parking lot of the Globe Hotel Las Vegas earlier in the summer.

"My name's Mike," the boy continued, "and, Lucas, you made us a promise and you kept it."

Lucas nodded cautiously. He decided he could possibly get a ride from these guys if he played nice.

"I always keep a promise," Lucas said.

"That's why we're here," said Mike. "We need a safe place to go to."

Astrid slapped her palm on the water. "We're not really in a position to help out right now," she said, "if you didn't happen to notice."

"The Good Company is broke, and everyone is trying get away from Ms. Günerro," Mike said. "We'll help you, if you help us."

"How exactly are *you* supposed to help us?" Astrid asked.

"We have Jet Skis, if *you* didn't happen to notice," Mike said, "and you have about two kilometers to swim back to shore."

"How did you know we were out here?" Kerala asked.

"We've been watching you all day," Mike said, pointing at the eight other boys on Jet Skis.

There was a pause for a second.

"Hop on," Mike said, "and we'll take you back to your van."

CHAPTER TWELVE

It was clear Mike was being honest, at least for the moment. The kids climbed aboard the Jet Skis, and the Curukians escorted Cesar and the New Resistance team back to shore in less than fifteen minutes.

It was noon when they got to the beach. The bow of Cesar's boat had been plowed into the middle of a kid's sand castle, and one of the tires on Cesar's van had been slashed.

THICKER THAN BLOOD

Cesar Vantes circled his van three times, and then he hugged it and cried.

"I love this van," he said in four languages.

"Someone must not like you guys today," Mike said.

"I think we have a pretty good idea who that might be," Nalini said.

The New Resistance kids stood under a palm tree, their shorty wet suits still dripping water onto their sandy feet.

Astrid's eyebrows crinkled like she was confused or unhappy. She set her mask and fins in a pile at the base of the tree. After a minute of staring, she folded her arms and spoke to the boys who had just brought them in by Jet Ski.

"So, Mike," she said skeptically. "How do we know you're not working with the Curukian girls who just tried to . . . um . . . kill us?"

Lucas nodded. He liked the tone Astrid was using. He was probably too trusting of people sometimes.

Cesar opened the back of the van and took out a jack.

"We're all Curukians," Mike said. "Or at least we used to be. We're not brainwashed anymore, but we need help getting out of the Good Company. That's why we need a safe place."

"What about these guys?" Kerala asked. "They don't speak?"

"Not English or Spanish or Catalan," Mike said. "All these guys are from Papua."

"Papua?" Travis said. "Indonesia or New Guinea?"

"Indonesia," Mike said. "They broke free earlier this year and trekked across Asia and Europe. We've been trying to get your attention all summer long to help us."

"What do you mean?" Astrid asked "Our attention?"

"We first met Lucas in the parking lot at the Globe Hotel in Las Vegas," Mike said. "Then Hervé tried to tell you in Paris and in Rome that brainwashing doesn't work, or at least not for that long." He paused. "You know Hervé Piveyfinaus, right?"

"Yeah," Astrid said. "He shows up everywhere."

"He's here," Mike said.

"Here?" Travis asked. "In Barcelona?"

"Yes," Mike said. "Hervé is organizing all the boys worldwide who want to leave the Good Company."

"How? Terry asked.

"With this new group of Curukian girls," Mike explained, "everyone has forgotten about the boys. And now the boys are waking up and thinking for themselves for the first time, and we know what we want."

"Let me get this straight," Alister asked. "So now

there are Good Company kids, ex-Curukians, all over the world who want to start over? Is that what you're saying?"

"Yes. Exactly."

Cesar closed the back doors of his van, slid the jack under the chassis, and began pumping the handle.

"What about you?" Kerala asked. "Do you have a home to go back to?"

Mike said, "You know the expression 'blood is thicker than water'?"

"It means," Nalini said, "that family, your blood, is more important than others."

"Right," Mike said. "Well, I have no family, and Ms. Günerro has pretty much ruined my whole childhood. So I had to start over. For me friends are my blood, my family."

"I have no family either," said Kerala, looking at the New Resistance kids. "But I have great friends."

"Sometimes all you need is a friend," said Mike.

Nalini opened the back of the van and grabbed the crate of shoes and T-shirts. Standing there on the sidewalk, the kids stripped off their wet suits.

In a matter of minutes, they were dressed in their flag swimsuits, white T-shirts, and tennis shoes.

Lucas thought they looked like a perfectly nerdy tourist group with matching uniforms.

"And you want us to help?" Nalini asked. "Is that right?"

"Yes," Mike said. "All of us."

"What about these Curukian girls?" Astrid asked. "Who are they?"

"Sometimes I don't even think they're human," Mike said. "But Ms. Günerro and Ms. T call them the newest and most beautiful weapon in the Good Company arsenal."

"What do you call them?" Terry asked.

"I don't call them," Mike said. "I run from them."

Mike then said something in Indonesian to the other boys, and they grumbled and nodded.

While the ex-Curukians talked, Jackknife crawled into the van and brought out a tray of bocadillo sandwiches, and everyone ate. After a minute Mike broke the silence.

He asked, "So, Lucas, you must not have told the Curukian girls what the message meant?"

"I didn't know the answer," Lucas said. "It's a riddle."

Astrid asked, "Why do you ask, Mike?"

"Well," Mike said, "Ms. Günerro said that if you didn't know what it meant, then your mother was a liar and she was trying to trick everyone about a treasure."

Lucas wanted to punch something. He hated it when someone said something bad about his mother.

"I don't understand," Travis asked. "There is or there isn't some valuable treasure somewhere? Which is it?"

Mike looked around nervously. "All I know," he said, "is that if Lucas didn't know about the priceless treasure, then Ms. Günerro was going to plan B."

"What's plan B?" Travis asked.

"Ms. Günerro and her partner now plan to steal a painting that they *think* is more valuable than priceless."

"What partner?" Travis asked. "She's not married."

Mike said, "Some super-rich guy named Ching Ching in Southeast Asia who sent Ms. Günerro a note with secret instructions."

"How do you know all of this?" Astrid asked.

Mike said, "The boy who does room service at the Good Hotel Barcelona, Andrés, took a picture of a note he delivered to Ms. Günerro this morning."

"What was the message?" Lucas asked.

"I couldn't understand it," Mike said. "But Hervé thinks there is a connection between Ching Ching's note and Lucas's mother's message."

"Is there?" Lucas asked.

"I don't know," Mike said. "That's why we need to work together."

"Can you get us a copy of the note?" Travis asked.

Mike said, "Hervé already sent a copy to the new butler at the Globe Hotel."

"Let's go then," Lucas said.

Alister leaned down and grabbed his briefcase and muttered something to Cesar whose feet were sticking out from under the van.

"He said he loves his van," Alister translated, "and he's staying with it while we go back to the hotel."

"Sounds like we're on our own," Nalini said, slipping a beach bag over her shoulder.

"Which way, Map Boy?" Astrid asked.

"The easiest way," Lucas said, "would be to catch a crosstown at that bus stop just south and west of us and then take the metro to the hotel."

"I don't have any money," Terry said.

"Don't worry," Astrid said. "Robbie gave me a prepaid card."

The kids said adios to Cesar and cut across the street. Mike and his group of eight ex-Curukians followed, wearing no shirts, wet cut-off jeans, and flip-flops.

Lucas looked back at Mike and the other boys. They smiled. They seemed to understand exactly what was going on. Lucas hoped he wasn't making a mistake by trusting them.

BUSLOAD OF CURUKIANS

At the bus stop, Mike's Indonesian friends squeezed onto a bench made for five.

Astrid, Nalini, and Kerala plopped down onto the concrete next to Jackknife. Terry and Alister leaned against the glass enclosure.

Nalini and Kerala tried speaking different languages with the boys to see if they could connect. The ex-Curukians spoke softly, and Nalini only knew a few greetings in Indonesian.

While they tried to talk, Lucas checked the bus schedule. He cupped his hand over his eyebrows to block the glare.

Mike looked over his shoulder. "Thanks," he said.

"For what?" Lucas asked.

"Keeping your promise. And for helping us get out of the Good Company."

"Well," Lucas said, "we're not out of the woods yet."

"We're not," Mike said, gesturing toward the ex-Curukians leaning against the bus stop. "But my group and I are a lot closer to getting out than the others."

"What others?"

Mike said, "There are a lot of kids in the world who

are forced to live and work in places they hate."

"Some kids have to go to schools they hate," Lucas quipped.

"True," Mike said. "But they wouldn't complain if they knew how bad it was for others, like us who come from poor countries."

An engine roared behind them.

A bus came around the corner and Lucas felt a sense of relief. They would be back at the hotel shortly. As the black bus angled into the curb, Mike grabbed Lucas's shoulder, squeezed, and pointed at the window.

This was definitely not a scheduled stop. The air brakes squeaked, and Lucas spotted the problem. Waiting in the bus's stairwell were eight girls with wet hair.

"Great," Mike said. "A busload of Curukians."

The Good Company bus idled as the front door opened.

Across the street a family loading beach gear into a Mercedes glanced over. A boy skateboarded down the opposite sidewalk as the eight girls got off the bus.

Mike barked something in Indonesian at the ex-Curukian boys. They sprang from the bench they had been sitting on and stood at attention. Blue veins in their arms swelled.

Astrid, Jackknife, Nalini, and Kerala took the boys' seats while Alister, Travis, and Terry crawled under the bench to the other side of the glass enclosure.

From the back corner of the bus stop Lucas studied the girls. They weren't particularly big or muscular, but there was something in the way they stood that worried him. Their ice-blue eyes spelled trouble with an attitude.

The girls stood but didn't try to make themselves look bigger. Quite the contrary. As the bus motor idled behind them, the eight girls stepped back at an angle.

Smart move, Lucas thought.

The girls crouched ever so slightly. It was a defensive move that made the target area, their bodies, smaller.

These girls have the best weapon ever, Lucas thought. *Brains.*

For half a minute the Curukian girls faced off against Mike and his ex-Curukians. No one said anything. It was a staring contest.

Someone was about to get hurt. It didn't take long for the primitive part of Lucas's brain to remind him that these girls standing in front of the bus stop had just cut off his air supply underwater. These girls were so brainwashed that they would do anything, even kill, and not think about it. This was the real deal. No one was cracking jokes.

Mike stepped forward, looking like a sergeant in the army.

He barked a one-word command in Indonesian to his eight Curukians.

CHAPTER FOURTEEN

The boys moved forward, and eight Curukian girls leaped at them, launching a combination of swinging kicks to the gut. The big Indonesian boys tried to swat them away, but the girls were too quick. Two girls jabbed two of the boys in the eyes, then followed up with massive elbow blows to the stomach. As the boys fell forward, the girls pinched the boys' necks and dropped them to the ground.

Lucas and the New Resistance stayed back in the safety of the closed-in bus stop. Alister, Terry, and Travis looked ready to run.

Three of the ex-Curukian boys tried to kick the girls, but they grabbed the boys' legs, straddled them, and spun them onto the concrete. The other boys had no chance. They were pummeled with a series of rapid-fire punches to the head, chest, and stomach. In less than fifteen seconds, the ex-Curukians lay sprawled across the curb, their feet splayed out into the street.

Mike crouched down to his friends.

"Don't touch them," said the girl with white hair. She seemed to be the spokesperson for the group.

"Ms. Günerro sends you a message," she said to Mike. "She says that you're well trained, and now is the time to switch back and double-cross your new best friend, Lucas Benes."

Lucas and the other New Resistance kids stared at Mike.

I'm such a fool, Lucas thought. *You can't always believe people.*

"Bleach, I've known you for a long time," Mike said. "We trained together in Bangladesh as kids, but I'm sick and tired of people telling me who I am supposed to be."

Bleach perched her foot on one of the boys' chests. The other girls copied her. They shifted their cold blue eyes toward Mike.

Mike recoiled and stood near Lucas inside the bus stop enclosure.

Bleach turned her attention to Lucas. "Since you're alive," she said, "I guess we'll give you one more chance."

Lucas's palms sweated.

Bleach continued the interrogation she had begun underwater. "What did your mother mean by 'more valuable than priceless'?"

The last time Lucas had told these girls that he didn't know, they had tried to kill him.

Seeing how quickly the girls had wrecked the Indonesian boys, Lucas's survival instincts decided this was not a fight moment but a time for flight.

Unfortunately, running away was not an option since they were boxed in by the glass bus stop behind them and by the Curukian girls in front.

Lucas opened his mind and immediately saw the problem. This whole time these girls had been staring at him without moving at all. Not because they thought he was a supermodel with bed-head hair. No. These girls used focus as their weapon, but it was also their weakness. It seemed that they could only concentrate on one thing at a time.

A distraction would give Lucas and friends the window of time they needed. But Lucas was at a loss for ideas. He eyed Astrid and Nalini.

Nalini seemed to read Lucas's lost look.

"Bleach," Nalini said. "That is your name, right?"

"It is."

"First," Nalini said, "I love your friends' two-tone black-and-white hairstyle, and then yours is so bold!"

"Thank you," Bleach said. "We take pride in our looks."

Astrid asked, "So the other girls don't speak?"

"Only in private," Bleach explained. "Girls like myself with single-color hair are the only ones Ms. Günerro allows to speak in public for the group."

"Please do tell us," Nalini said. "Where are you all from?"

"What do you mean," Bleach asked, "where are we from?"

"And don't say you're from Raffish, Curuk," Jackknife said.

"She means," Astrid said, "are you French or Chinese or Russian?"

"We're none of those," Bleach said. "We're vegetarians."

For the first time the Curukian girls smiled, as if proud.

The front and back doors of the bus suddenly

opened. Four huge, hairy men dressed in uniforms stepped onto the sidewalk and opened the luggage doors at the bottom of the tour bus.

Lucas spotted someone inside scrambling out the other side.

The men lifted the beaten-up Indonesian boys like heavy duffel bags and tossed them into the luggage compartment.

Next the men grabbed Mike and shoved him in with the others. As soon the hairy guys had boarded the bus, a strange sulfur smell began to drift in the air.

Moments later, smoke billowed out from the luggage compartment. Within a few seconds a thick gray cloud covered the entire area, completely hiding the bus.

The Curukian girls turned and faced the smoke, mesmerized.

A split second later a bald-headed boy wearing khakis and a golf shirt cut through the fog. Using a wooden cane, Hervé Piveyfinaus limped past the dazed Curukian girls and straight up to Astrid.

"Hervé?" she asked. "You're really here?"

"But of course," Hervé said.

AN OLD FRIEND

Hervé Piveyfinaus wafted the smoke away and gave Astrid a kiss on both cheeks. He went around to the group and shook hands with the others.

"Don't worry about Bleach and her Curukian clique," said Hervé with a thick French accent. "They are in a trance."

"What do you mean?" Travis asked, pointing at the Curukian girls. "A trance?"

"They hate fire," Hervé said. "Smoke freezes their minds. It was part of their original brainwashing ceremony."

Lucas glanced over at the Curukian girls. They were just standing there like statues facing the smoke, their hands raised to the sky. The girls were frozen by fire.

"We must hurry," Hervé said. "Deception for Bleach and her girls only lasts a short time." He turned and pointed with his cane. "If you would, please. Follow me and walk this way."

"What about Mike and the other boys?" Lucas asked.

"Save yourself first," Hervé said. "Mike and his team are wounded and will only slow you down."

The French kid limped past the almost lifeless girls who seemed unaware that anything was going on.

The New Resistance kids did as they were told and followed Hervé into the cloud of smoke.

Hervé led the New Resistance kids down the street and away from the bus. They turned left and soon crossed a promenade filled with trees and sculptures, and on the other side Hervé stopped them.

"The smoke will clear soon," he said, "and Bleach and her girls will wake up, and they will hunt us down."

As fast as they could, Hervé and the New Resistance kids took off running through the streets of Barcelona.

LA RAMBLA

A zoo is normally a refuge for animals, but today the Barcelona Zoo became a refuge for children.

When Hervé and the New Resistance kids got to the entrance, Astrid and the girls went straight to the booth to buy tickets.

The boys huddled in the shade of a plane tree. The sudden return of the French boy was clearly at the top of everyone's mind.

"Hervé," Jackknife said. "What's your deal? You just appear and disappear?"

"Stealth is my strength," Hervé said. "You must believe me. I am here to help."

"Did someone give you a note this morning?" Lucas asked.

Hervé said, "Andrés gave me a picture he had taken of a message from Ching Ching to Ms. Günerro."

"What did it say?" Travis asked.

"It made no sense," Hervé said. "I delivered it to Mr. Chapman at your hotel."

"You were at our hotel today?" Jackknife asked.

"Yes," Hervé said. "The Globe Hotel was crazy. The police were talking to Charles Magnus who was crying like a baby. And that's how I knew to find you at the beach."

The boys paused a moment and digested the news. Travis still seemed skeptical.

"What are you really doing here?" Travis asked.

Hervé asked, "Do you remember when I told you that brainwashing doesn't always work?"

"*I* certainly do," Jackknife said.

"Since the Good Company is losing so much money," Hervé explained, "no one is getting re-brainwashed. Now everyone wants to be free."

"That's all anyone wants," Alister said as he straightened his bow tie.

"What about those girls?" Travis asked. "The one named Bleach."

"Ms. T made her terrible," Hervé said. "But smoke and fire were used in their brainwashing ceremonies as a form of hypnosis. It is a weakness for these girls."

Alister asked, "Did you start a fire back there at the bus?"

"Smoke bomb," Hervé said. "Hundreds of them from the Good factory in China where my father was . . . well . . ."

Terry turned and pointed. "They're here."

The Good Company bus they had just run away from was pulling into the zoo parking lot.

Lucas glanced at the slow ticket line. He calculated the time and distance, and it was clear Bleach would arrive before Astrid got tickets.

"We've got no time," Lucas said, racing toward the zoo entrance.

"Hurry!" Terry yelled to the girls in line.

Astrid, Kerala, and Nalini dropped out of line and sprinted to the entrance. One by one the kids hurdled the turnstiles and entered the park.

Just on the inside a policeman folded his arms and stared them down.

The Good Company bus pulled up to the curb, and the door opened. A clump of Curukian girls marched in a line straight for the zoo entrance.

The policeman approached Lucas.

Lucas said to him in Spanish, "Those girls are vegetarians; they are coming here to release all the animals."

"¿Verdad?" the policeman asked.

"True," said Alister.

The policeman blew his whistle, and he was joined by two more officers. The cops stopped the vegetarians at the gate.

The New Resistance kids didn't stay around to see how things played out for the Curukian girls.

Like an international cross-country running team they jogged together into the zoo.

Peacocks fluttered out of their way. They sped around the cages of lions, hippo baths, and giraffe exhibits. They didn't stop until Jackknife spotted a bank of vending machines.

"I'm thirsty and starving," he said.

Nalini popped him on the head. "You have worms in your stomach."

"I have nothing in my stomach," Jackknife said. "That's why I'm hungry."

They kept moving through the crowd of people watching monkeys swing from ropes. Jackknife took the lead, and the others fell in line. They left the zoo and sprinted down a gravel path lined with trees and flowers. Finally, they exited the park through a pair of giant wrought-iron gates and stepped back into the busy city.

The streets were jam-packed with tourists and taxis, and one big black bus.

"They're back!" Terry said.

"This way," Lucas said, recalibrating the map in his head.

They crossed Picasso Street, where nearly every building and van had been tagged with graffiti. Lucas actually thought it looked pretty cool, but they didn't dare stop.

In the next block the air smelled sweet, and soon they found themselves standing in front of the Museum of Chocolate.

"Let's go here," Jackknife said. "I love chocolate."

"Everyone loves chocolate," Hervé said as he stopped and leaned on his cane.

"Lucas," Nalini said. "Lead."

"I remember," Lucas said, "seeing on a map that there's a Vespa shop just around the corner."

"Show us the way," said Travis.

"Bus!" Terry said. "Nine o'clock."

The group stopped and huddled around Hervé for a second.

"How far to the hotel, Lucas?" Kerala asked.

"On foot," he said, "probably an hour, maybe an hour and a half if we have to zigzag our way back through these tiny streets."

"Perfect," said Nalini. "A bus can't make it through all these streets."

"Great idea," Lucas said as he turned the other way.

They moved through the neighborhood, down streets so narrow that a Smart car couldn't squeeze through. They zipped past the Picasso Museum, digging deeper into a maze of cobblestone lanes, cafés, card shops, and cathedrals. In a few minutes they crossed the Plaça Reial, the royal plaza, where it must have been near two o'clock in the afternoon, since the waiters at the outdoor restaurants were clearing the tables from lunch.

Jackknife drooled at a table filled with half-eaten plates of sausage, bread, and tomatoes. Nalini and Kerala pushed him along.

In a few minutes they came to the most famous street in all of Barcelona.

La Rambla.

The Spanish poet Garcia Lorca said that La Rambla was "the only street in the world which I wish would never end."

For Lucas and friends, it was a dead end. The wide avenue was packed with tourists, shoppers, pickpockets, and a dozen girls marching straight at them. The Curukians came from everywhere.

"Where's Hervé?" Travis asked.

They looked around.

"He's gone," Astrid said.

Bleach and her clique moved closer.

Behind Lucas there was a space between two buildings. It was the only way out. The kids turned sideways and shimmied down the narrow passage. The Curukian girls squeezed in and followed.

When Lucas got to the end of the alley, a bus door opened in his face.

The driver said, "All aboard."

TOURISTS TOUR

With the New Resistance kids on board, the Good Company bus toured through the city.

Bleach and the Curukian girls sat up front, and the hairy goons took the backseats.

Lucas sat in the middle row next to Jackknife. He lay his head on the window and let the air conditioning blow through his hair and dry his sweat.

"Where do you think we're going?" Jackknife asked.

Astrid was sitting right behind them. "Knowing what I know about Ms. Günerro," she said, "there's only one place she would be."

"What do you mean?" Alister asked.

"Everything is opposite with this lady," Astrid explained. "She doesn't treat anything or anyone with respect. So to me, she would go to the last place you would think an evil person would go."

"Where?" Terry asked from across the aisle.

"Well," Lucas said, "we're headed northwest, away from the water."

"She's going to be in church," Travis said. "Isn't she?"

"What!" Alister said. "Are we talking about the same person?"

"You weren't there, Alister," Astrid said. "But in Paris we found Ms. Günerro at the Notre Dame Cathedral dressed up as a priest."

"What!" Alister said again.

"Astrid's right," Lucas said. "They're taking us to the Sagrada Família."

"What's that?" Terry asked.

Kerala said, "The translation is 'Sacred Family' or 'Holy Family.'"

"Meaning like, um, God?" Terry asked.

"It's a church, dude," Jackknife said. "Yes, meaning like, um, God."

"It's a massive place," Travis explained, "that looks like a cathedral. And it is, in a good way, the freakiest-looking building you'll ever see."

"It's still not even finished yet, is it?" Nalini asked.

"Construction was started in the 1880s," Travis explained. "It's the masterpiece of the famous architect Gaudí. I'm actually excited we're going."

"Travis," Jackknife said. "We don't need a history lesson about everything."

"But," Terry asked, "the church is not even done yet?"

"Not finished," Nalini said.

"We might all be finished," Astrid said, "if we don't come up with something quick."

In a short while the bus stopped next to the playground across the street from the world-famous Sagrada Família. The huge, hairy men and the Curukian girls escorted Lucas and the New Resistance kids off the bus and into the park.

The massive church rose up before them. The kids gawked as they walked. It was as big as a cathedral but with spires that looked like giant, drippy sand castles. Construction cranes screeched overhead looking as if they were a natural part of the church itself.

Lucas took inventory. Literally tons of construction material—scaffolding, elevators, and trucks.

Hundreds of tourists clustered in groups outside the church. Like teachers on a field trip, the men marched the kids to the front doors. The entranceway looked like someone had stuck statues into a giant candle of melted wax.

One of the men handed Bleach some tickets. "We'll wait here," he said.

Bleach and her Curukian girls sandwiched Lucas and friends as they entered the church.

The New Resistance kids looked up and down and spun around, bumping into one another as they marveled at the sheer size of the place. It was like being in a forest where the columns were giant trees that branched out.

People shuffled everywhere. Some tourists listened to headsets; others ambled around taking pictures and looking at guidebooks. From some corner of the church a woman sang, her voice filling the cavernous interior.

Lucas was particularly excited by the geometric

shapes. There were double twisted columns, hyperboloids, and spiral staircases. It was the most wildly beautiful place he had ever seen.

Until . . .

Until he saw Ms. Siba Günerro, standing with Goper and Ekki and six new Curukian girls with half-black, half-white hair.

SAGRADA FAMÍLIA

A dozen Curukian girls corralled Lucas and the New Resistance kids and pushed them into a circle with Ms. Günerro. A few tour groups shuffled past their circle, and as they did, Terry Hines slipped out and crawled under a pew.

"Well, well, well," Ms. Günerro said to Lucas. "We meet again. In this beautiful church, no less. You do like the place?"

Lucas nodded. "It's nice."

"I'm hoping they let me play the organ," she said. "What do you think?"

Astrid wasted no time in arguing with Ms. Günerro. "No one wants to hear you play anything. That's what we think."

Ms. Günerro asked, "Are you Lucas's lawyer now?"

"No," Astrid said. "I'm his sister. *And* his friend."

Nalini stepped forward. "And so am I."

"If I may?" Bleach asked.

Ms. Günerro said, "Go ahead."

"I never let go of a question once I've asked it," Bleach said. "And I've asked Lucas twice, and I still haven't gotten an answer. So may I ask again?"

"Please," Ms. Günerro said. "We're in church. Ask

until you receive an answer."

Bleach turned to Lucas. "What is more valuable than priceless?"

"Don't answer," Astrid said. She turned to Ms. Günerro. "You know, you're just not a good person. You should not even be in a church. It's sacrilegious for you to even walk in here. Like when you were at Notre Dame and you had that ridiculous air-conditioned dress. You don't have respect for anything. You don't even know what is valuable."

Ms. Günerro pursed her lips.

"On second thought," Astrid continued, "maybe you should spend more time in a church. But what you really need to do is quit being such an awful person ruining other people's lives just so your company can make even more money. What you need to do is—"

"What you need to do, young lady," Ms. Günerro said, her voice frigid, "is close your mouth."

Astrid's shoulders dropped.

"Enough with the lawyer talk," Ms. Günerro said. "We are only here to discuss one thing."

Nalini stepped forward and took Astrid's place. "Do tell us that one thing!" she said, acting as if she and Ms. Siba Günerro were best friends.

The Curukian girls' ice-blue eyes locked on Nalini. Ms. Günerro shifted her focus.

Maybe Ms. Günerro is like the Curukian girls, Lucas thought. *She, too, can only focus on one thing at a time.*

CHAPTER EIGHTEEN

"The one thing we want to know," Bleach explained, "is what is more valuable than priceless? That's all we want to know!"

Kerala leaned in. "Who really wants to know?" she asked.

Death by Middle School had begun.

Again the girls' eyes shifted, and Ms. Günerro's, too.

"I got this one," Ekki said. "Ching Ching has instructed Ms. Günerro to—"

Goper backhanded Ekki in the belly.

"Why do all the girls have to speak for Lucas? Is he hiding something?" Goper asked.

Travis, Jackknife, and Alister stepped forward.

"Isn't priceless an absolute?" Travis asked. "Meaning that you can't modify it with an adverb."

Everyone's eyes glazed over.

"It can't be *more* priceless," Jackknife said. "Can it?"

"That would be like . . ." Alister said. "You know, it's like saying 'very unique' or 'completely destroyed.'"

The Curukian girls looked to Ms. Günerro.

"What my friends mean," Travis said, "is more than priceless is actually impossible. You know! If it is price-*less*, then it doesn't have a price, so you can't have something that is more than not having a something."

"It's like . . ." Alister added. "It's like saying 'the most infinity.'"

"Or like opposite day," Jackknife said. "How do you know when is opposite day? If it's opposite day, it could already be opposite of opposite, which would be very confusing."

"I know what this is," Bleach said, throwing her hands up in the air. "This is a bunch of Americans trying to avoid the question."

"I'm no bloody American," Alister said. "I'm Scottish, and I live in the Falklands!"

"I'm Indian," Nalini said, "as in from India."

"What?" Bleach asked. "Why do you speak English with a British accent?"

"Because the English colonized India."

"Brazilian," Jackknife deadpanned. "Thank you very much."

"Enough!" Ms. Günerro said. "I'm frustrated yet again with a group of Benes brats."

Bleach's eyes pleaded with Lucas. "Just tell Ms. Günerro what the message means."

"I know exactly what it means," Lucas said. "And where the treasure is hidden."

No one in the circle moved. Lines of tourists shuffled past the group, insulating them from the rest of the church.

"He's lying," Ms. Günerro said to Bleach. "Take Lucas and his friends on the bus to our hotel basement. Ms. T is starting a hotel-school for kids, and she would love to teach Lucas all about treasures."

Ms. Günerro turned to Goper and Ekki. "Plan A is over," she said. "Let's start plan B."

UP IS THE NEW OUT

The CEO of the Good Company turned and locked arms with Ekki and Goper. The threesome strolled down the main aisle of the church and disappeared through another entranceway.

From the corner of his eye, Lucas could see Terry Hines signaling behind an iron gate.

Bleach and her girls pushed the New Resistance kids toward the front doors.

Lucas nudged Astrid.

"Do something," he whispered.

As they rounded a collection of kneelers, Astrid stopped the group.

"Bleach," she said. "Let's talk, shall we?"

All twelve Curukian girls shifted their focus to Astrid.

"Does anyone have a makeup mirror?" Astrid asked.

"No," Bleach said. "Why do you ask?"

Nalini dug in her beach bag and placed a compact in Astrid's hand.

"Okay," Astrid said. "So I have to tell you I love the outfits. Rompers are my favorites, and that yellow is to die for."

"What are you trying to do?" Bleach asked. "Distract us?"

"No, not at all," Astrid said. "I just wanted to ask you what kind of makeup you use? I love it."

Bleach grinned. "Good makeup, of course."

"I just thought I would tell you . . ." Astrid leaned in and whispered, "Your mascara is running."

Astrid flicked open the makeup case and handed it to Bleach. The other girls huddled around the tiny mirror to check their eyes.

Astrid took one step back, and the New Resistance kids fell in line, following Lucas between two pews. They cut around a column and beelined it straight for the spiral staircase.

Terry flung open the gate and said, "Up is the new out."

The kids followed Terry into the stairwell. They ran up the spiral staircase two steps at a time. Tourists streamed down the steps, but Lucas and friends charged up, pushing people out of their way.

A moment later they heard Bleach and her girls calling out from below.

Midway up Kerala stopped a group of Italian tourists. "Stop the girls in the yellow outfits, please," she said in Italian.

Out of breath the New Resistance kids burst through the door and onto the roof. The sky was brilliant blue and sun baked. Construction safety wire surrounded them.

Nalini panted. "Now what are we going to do?"

The view from the top of the Sagrada Família was

awesome—all of Barcelona at their feet with the Mediterranean Sea in the distance. Lucas looked down at the tiny people on the square.

"Three hundred and seventy two feet," Lucas muttered. "One hundred and thirteen meters."

Lucas looked up at the construction cranes sailing above their heads.

"Don't even think about it," Astrid said. "We are not using those cranes to get us off this roof."

"I'm not," Lucas said. "When we were coming in, I spotted a construction elevator on the other side. Come on."

The New Resistance kids followed Lucas around the roof of the church, through the metal ramps, until they came to a locked door for the construction zone. On the other side men in dirty white T-shirts sawed blocks of stone.

Alister knelt and sized up the lock and chain. He took the key kit from his briefcase and started picking.

Rising above their heads were spires topped with ornaments of oranges, grapes, and bananas. More of Gaudí's incredible style.

Jackknife stared at the fruit. "This is making me hungry."

Nalini shook her head. "You need a doctor."

The lock clicked, and Alister stripped the chain through the gate and opened it.

Bleach and a handful of Curukian girls blasted

through a group of tourists and sprinted across the roof.

"Go, go, go!" Alister called to the others as he slammed the gate closed and threaded the chain back through it. As soon as he clicked the lock, Bleach and two other girls smashed into the fence, knocking Alister back.

"Got another lock over here," Jackknife called back to Alister.

Nalini, Terry, and Astrid were inspecting the elevator when a group of construction workers in hard hats approached them.

"*¿Qué pasa?*" they asked. "What's going on?"

Lucas spoke to them in Spanish. "Those girls," he said, pointing toward Bleach, "are stealing artwork from the church."

"What are you doing then?" said a man with a beard.

"We're going to get the police," Astrid said. "You guys stop those girls."

The men hurried toward the Curukian girls.

Alister picked the lock on the elevator, and the kids crammed into the tiny cage. They clanked down and in a few minutes stepped onto the sidewalk.

Jackknife pointed at the scuba van parked across the street, a spare tire on the back wheel. "That's weird," he said.

Lucas didn't really care how strange it was that Cesar Vantes had somehow followed them to the Sagrada Família. He cut through the traffic and the others followed and they piled into the back of the scuba van.

"How'd you know we were here?" Kerala asked Cesar.

"I took a guess that if the Good Company caught up with you," Cesar said, "Ms. Günerro would have you brought here. Cesar looked through the windshield. "See! There she is right there, walking this way."

SAFE AND SOUND

"Duck," Astrid commanded.

The New Resistance kids hit the floor of the van and lay still as Cesar slowly pulled out of his parking spot and motored past the Sagrada Família. They rounded the playground across the street from the church and Lucas stuck his head up front.

"Stop," he said.

Lucas hopped out of the van and ran over to the Good Company bus. He paused behind a palm tree to make sure the coast was clear. Then he ran up to the back of the bus, slid down the side, and flipped open the luggage compartments.

The ex-Curukian boys rolled out, holding their stomachs.

Mike stood up and said, "Thanks."

"Let's go," Lucas said.

"These guys can't move right now," Mike said. "You go on without us."

Lucas glanced at the boys. They were in no shape to move fast. Lucas knew that if they were caught with the New Resistance, then Ms. Günerro would know for sure they were traitors.

"If you really want to join the New Resistance,"

Lucas said, "come to the Globe Hotel Barcelona after midnight and check in with Coach Creed or Rufus Chapman."

"Perfect," Mike said. "We'll hide until midnight."

Lucas split and made his way back to the van.

Cesar drove through the stone streets and past Gaudí's Park Güell, and in a few minutes everyone was back at the hotel.

Safe and sound.

One of the best things about being at this particular hotel-school was the lack of adult supervision.

For Jackknife, his fixation was of course the one thing Coach Creed had forbidden: the maze of tubes and slides that spanned the giant swimming pool.

"Thanks for the field trip today, guys," Jackknife said as he climbed out of the van. "But I have some forbidden fun with my name on it."

Jackknife gathered up a few kids who were swimming and ran toward the slide.

Nalini, Astrid, and Kerala found the best broken lounge chairs they could find and pulled them together.

Lucas stood behind them hoping no one would notice him. There was no way he was going to get in the pool.

Jackknife and a group of boys scrambled up a rickety ladder that led to the main tube.

This was no typical backyard pool slide. It was a

towering network of intertwined tubes, a jungle gym that snaked back and forth in a series of neck-cracking turns.

"This looks so awesome," Jackknife said as he stood at the top of the structure.

Travis grabbed the ladder's handle, and the corroded bar cracked, snapped off, and clattered to the ground.

"Whoops," he said.

Rust covered every piece of metal on the entire slide. Coach Creed was right. This wasn't a good idea.

"Come on!" Jackknife called from the top of the structure.

Peer pressure was always terrible. Lucas thought about leaving and going back up to his room. But then again, the slide did look kind of fun.

"Come on, Lucas," Jackknife said again. "Don't be chicken."

By the time the boys had reached the top of the ladder, a crowd of other students had come out of the hotel and gathered around the deck. Kids were lining up to go down the slide.

Lucas knew deep down that he shouldn't go. What he wanted was time by himself to think. That's what he really needed.

But maybe . . . he thought.

He figured he would go once, and everyone would leave him alone. While they were swimming, he would slip away unnoticed to his room and go to sleep.

Jackknife twisted a faucet and the rusted handle cracked and sprang a leak, spewing water over the platform where they stood.

As the water flowed down into the pool, Jackknife loaded himself luge style into the first tube. He rocked back and forth in the stream of water, then launched himself down the slide. The plastic tubes shook and rattled the whole network.

While Jackknife's yelps filled the air, Lucas noticed that several rivets holding the slide sections together were missing. If he were ever going to go, it would be now before the whole thing collapsed.

Jackknife sliced into the pool, and when he came up, he flung his hair to the side and let out a giant whoop.

"Watch out for turn three," he said, rubbing his arm. "There are some sharp edges."

"Great," Travis said as he adjusted the spigot to force more spray into the second tube.

The entire maze of slides screeched and groaned as more and more kids climbed up and jumped in.

Sopping wet, Alister and Travis grabbed Lucas and practically pulled him up the slide. The threesome went at the same time in different tubes.

As he was rocketing through the tube, Lucas spotted beams of light flickering through the cracked plastic. He heard a series of metal groans, and then he felt the tube tilting.

Alister, Lucas, and Travis shot out of the tubes and into the pool.

Jackknife climbed on top of the structure and stood like an Olympic diver. He sprang up, touched his toes, and knifed into the water.

The moment he jumped from the platform, everyone heard the noise.

From the deep end Lucas treaded water and looked up. The maze of chutes and ladders creaked. The beast twisted and leaned toward the pool. Then, in one explosive crash, the entire slide and its ladder network careened into the pool with a giant splash.

Lucas, Alister, and Travis ducked underwater.

The metal and plastic buried the boys.

Lucas opened his eyes, and bromine rushed in like fire. He started to swim up, but the metal maze had pinned his legs to the bottom of the pool. When he pushed, a ladder jabbed him in the shin.

While Lucas was contemplating his second near drowning in the same day, Astrid and Nalini dove into the water. Up top Lucas could see Coach Creed yelling down into the pool. The girls stood on both sides of Lucas and lifted the slide just enough for him to squirm out.

Mr. Benes was waiting poolside with Coach Creed when they got out. The grown-ups had obviously heard the slide crashing.

We are in so much trouble, Lucas thought.

But getting in trouble in a group was always

better than by yourself.

Coach Creed breathed deeply and spoke to the kids. His Texas accent was thicker than normal.

"What baffles me," he said, "is that kids as smart as you all are can manage to do things far beyond the borders of stupid."

He stopped talking and let the word *stupid* float in the air for a while. Lucas knew they had been irresponsible, and it made him feel awful.

"We're not going to punish you," Mr. Benes said, "because ultimately you have to live with your actions—good or bad. For your whole life. Which is why we want you to make good choices."

Everyone stared at the concrete.

Rufus Chapman clomped across the pool deck, the sound of his shoes breaking the silence. He was dressed in a newly pressed tuxedo, a white napkin draped over his arm. As Lucas got his first glimpse of the man, he thought he looked exactly like a British butler.

"Excuse me, everyone," Rufus said. "I've been a bit tied up, as they say." He paused and looked at Coach Creed. "Thank you again for rescuing me from that closet."

Coach nodded. "If we hadn't been looking for you, Rufus, we wouldn't have found Charles Magnus. And now that he and his team have turned themselves in to the police, we have the upper hand with the Good Company."

Jackknife pumped his arm. "Yes!"

"Indeed." Rufus said. "All things happen for a reason. It also happens to be suppertime, which is served presently in the main dining room."

Coach Creed turned and faced the kids. "After you eat," he said, "everyone in his or her room. We are on lockdown as of nine o'clock tonight. No exceptions."

No one said anything. They shuffled in shamed silence to the dining hall, where they ate mountains of the most delicious paella with chicken, shrimp, and octopus.

At the table Lucas decided that he had had enough of everything. He was going to take it easy and not get into any intense, dangerous, or life-threatening situations. Never again. He figured if he could just sleep for the rest of his life, everything would be okay.

That night, Lucas kept to his word.

After dinner he climbed the stairs to his room and showered and crawled into bed.

For the next fourteen hours Lucas crashed. He slept straight through the night and well into the next morning. While he dozed, dark clouds surrounded him as a nightmare populated with a new kind of Curukian invaded his mind. Girls with black-and-white hair came rushing at him and strangled him with ropes.

As he dug out of his nest of cords, he swam up through the dream and saw everyone at the New

CHAPTER TWENTY

Resistance pulling him up. Lucas woke. He didn't know exactly what it was, but in his heart he could feel what his mother meant by more valuable than priceless.

BASEMENT DISCOVERY

At the same time Lucas's sleep was turning fitful and dark, Travis Chase made an amazing discovery that would change everything. He had just seen an advertisement for a television program that he knew would rock the New Resistance.

First he needed some recording equipment to prove his point.

With his skateboard under his arm Travis rumbled down the back stairs of the hotel. At the first-floor landing he ran into Rufus Chapman, who seemed to be lost in thought.

"Hi, Rufus."

"Hello, Travis," Rufus said. "Where are you off to?"

"I'm going to copy a film that will help us find more kids who want to get away from the Good Company."

"Dear me," Rufus said. "We've been inundated with messages from kids all over the world."

"Did some Indonesian kids show up last night?"

"Oh yes," Rufus said. "At midnight exactly."

"Great."

Rufus said, "Mr. Benes may be issuing an alarm this morning."

"Oh, you mean a Call to Legs," Travis said.

CHAPTER TWENTY-ONE

"Where are we going?"

"Madrid."

"Where did we get that from?" Travis asked.

"From Andrés, a young man I trained over at the Good Hotel Barcelona. Apparently the guard named Ekki inadvertently leaked some information this morning."

Travis said, "This video I am going to record may actually change our destination."

"One can always change direction."

"True."

"Carry on then."

Travis descended the stairs and entered a dank and musty basement. He flicked on the overhead lights, and only one fluorescent bank lit up fully. The other fixtures hummed, casting spots of dull brown light.

Around him the concrete in the old hotel creaked. Travis moved toward a dark corner where the video equipment was located. Then he heard a voice.

"Travis?"

"Yeah?" he said into the black space. "Who's that?"

"Sora. Sora Kowa."

"What are you doing down here?"

"Meditating," she said. "What are you doing down here?"

"I'm looking for a machine," Travis said. "I've got to record a TV show."

"What show?"

"It's a BBC news program," he said. "It'll scare us all

to death. It's coming on at nine."

"In just a few minutes," Sora said, glancing at her watch. "I can help if you'd like."

"Thanks," he said. "Plug that TV in, would you?"

The television was clunky, and it sat on Cesar Vantes's paper-covered desk. Sora turned the TV on while Travis looked for something to record the show with. He clicked a lightbulb hanging above the messy workstation. A broken clock on the tool rack said the time was 4:17. There were all sorts of tools tossed around—hammers and wrenches and screwdrivers; dusty and rotted manuals; and cardboard boxes filled with colorful cables, wires, and cords. There was a long wooden rod holding different kinds of tape—masking, duct, electrical. Travis rifled through the junk and trash but found nothing.

Underneath this worktable Sora found a box with cassette tapes. She held up a rectangular plastic box shaped like a book and looked at it inquisitively.

"What's this?" she said.

"That looks like an old eight-track tape from the 1970s."

Travis flipped it over, and it showed a faded image of Andrés Segovia.

"I've actually never seen one of these," he said. "This one only has eight songs!"

"That's huge," Sora said. "For eight songs?"

Travis tossed the 8-track back into another box and spotted a bigger rectangular case—

thick, black, and plastic.

"That's a VHS!" Sora said. "For recording TV, isn't it?"

Travis remarked, "It's the same size as an e-reader."

He picked it up and looked at the spool of tape inside the case. "This thing is the reason older people always say 'tape it' when they really mean record it."

Sora laughed. "Let's find a machine that can 'tape' your show."

Travis opened a metal cabinet, looking for a machine that could record onto VHS. Inside there were stacks of cameras, microphones, and cassette recorders. On the bottom shelf, Travis spotted a VHS recorder. It was so big that at first he thought it was a microwave oven.

Sora said, "That's it."

Travis located the cables for the recorder and hooked it up to the TV.

The program he wanted to record came on the television with three BBC News beeps. The VHS machine blinked red, indicating that it was taping the show.

Travis and Sora watched the news with their mouths wide open. When the segment ended, Travis popped the tape out. He couldn't wait to show it to the others.

PLAN B

Travis Chase sprinted up the back staircase to the seventh floor. He flipped his skateboard onto the floor, and the wheels squished into the carpet that was still damp from Lucas playing firefighter with Magnus's face. The door to room 701 had been wedged open, and a bank of fans blew warm air into the hallway.

Travis glided down the seventh floor, where he thumped the nose of the longboard into the door as he burst into room 725.

Alister sprang up and guarded his hotel of cards. Lucas sat wide-eyed. Jackknife rolled over in his bed and burped.

Travis pushed across the carpet and glided to the foot of Lucas's bed.

"Let's roll," he said.

"Where are we going?" Jackknife said, not even looking up from his pillow.

"Madrid."

"As in the capital of Spain?" Alister asked.

Jackknife asked, "What's up?"

"Rufus has a mole of some kind, the kid named Andrés, at Ms. Günerro's hotel," Travis said. "Apparently plan B for the Good Company is in Madrid."

CHAPTER TWENTY-TWO

"Are *we* going?" Lucas asked.

"Your dad is going to issue a Call to Legs soon," Travis said.

"Do we have to go?" Jackknife asked.

"I'm happy staying right here in bed," Lucas said.

Alister said, "You've been asleep forever, Lucas."

"It doesn't matter," Travis said. "The trip is not optional."

Jackknife sat up. "Madrid's not that far away. We going by car or train?"

"Neither," Travis said. "White Bird One."

CHAPTER 23

WHITE BIRD ONE

An alarm pulsated in the hallway, and a yellow light flashed throughout the hotel.

"All members of the New Resistance," said a voice over the ceiling speakers. "This is a Call to Legs."

A CTL was like a fire drill, except that when you got out of the building, the mission started, and the chances of dying were infinitely greater.

In complete silence everyone filed out of the rooms, down the stairs, through the lobby, and onto the front circular drive of the hotel. Outside, a line of vans waited.

The kids piled in, and the drivers transported them to a private airfield north of Barcelona.

When they got out of the vans, the sun was hot and bright, and the sky was littered with parachuters.

Two airport technicians rolled open a giant hangar door. Inside, the Boeing 747 Intercontinental airliner dominated the space.

White Bird One.

Teams of workers buzzed across the floor on golf carts. Mechanics scurried around the airplane performing the final check. A fuel truck beeped as it backed up.

Lucas loved this airplane. Who wouldn't? It was arguably the most modern flying machine ever, tricked out with every luxury in the world. Paid for by the profits from his dad's chain of Globe Hotels.

As they shuffled toward the big plane, Lucas fantasized about sleeping in one of the calm blue pods and eating candy for hours on end.

The grown-ups walked in front of the kids.

"This is going to be a short flight," Mr. Benes said to the group. "So don't get too comfortable."

Coach Creed marched backward. "Eyes on me," he called out. "When we get on the plane, I want Tier One and Alister at the boardroom table, Tier Two on the sides, and everyone else in your pods. We're working with very little information, so we're counting on you to do a lot in a short amount of time."

The kids clomped up the back staircase and through the galley. Jackknife snatched a handful of snacks and Cokes and then stopped. He unclicked the food service cart and pushed it down the aisle toward the boardroom.

While a soft Spanish guitar drifted through the speakers, white LED lights on the ceiling faded into a pastel blue. As the kids approached the next compartment, a door slid open. Inside, a mahogany table took up the center of the oval-shaped boardroom.

A voice cut in and crackled over the intercom. "Please take your seats, and buckle those belts."

Jackknife locked the service trolley's wheels and

passed drinks and snacks across the table.

The other Tier One kids—Lucas, Astrid, Nalini, Travis, Kerala—and Alister crashed into the regular airplane seats that surrounded the table. A dozen other kids took the window seats and opened their laptops.

Lucas gazed out the rectangular windows and spotted the grown-ups huddled with the pilot. A flock of parakeets flew into the hangar and rested on the ceiling's metal trusses. At the back of the airplane Lucas heard Gini giggling.

It all started with her, he thought.

There was a little commotion as the rest of the kids took their seats. A few minutes later, the main cabin door closed.

Tug trucks pulled the airplane from the hangar and out onto the tarmac.

"Please prepare for takeoff," said Captain Bannister over the PA system.

The engines fired, and the plane rattled and shook as the all-white jet blasted down the runway. In less than two minutes the aircraft rocketed up into the blue Spanish sky. Soon they were fast approaching the speed of sound.

The seat-belt light dinged, and the two program leaders came down the circular stairs to start the meeting. They had obviously spent some time shopping while in Barcelona. Robbie Stafford wore a baby-blue suit and white T-shirt, and Sophia Carson followed wearing a pink pleated dress and carrying a tablet under her arm. The two fifth-year seniors took their seats at the head of the table.

"This flight will take only about an hour," Sophia said. "So, as Coach said, we have a lot to do in a short time."

Some kids grumbled.

Someone in the back of the plane called out, "Nothing to eat?"

"As some of you may have heard," Sophia went on, "we are headed to Madrid today. We have credible information that Ms. Günerro is planning an attack of some kind on one of Madrid's museums."

Robbie said, "Although Travis has a film that he says conflicts with this information."

"Which museum are we supposed to be going to?" Astrid asked.

"Good question," Sophia said. "We don't know exactly which one."

"Wait a minute," Jackknife said. "It seems to me that we should have already figured this out, you know. We're going to this big city but we don't know exactly where?"

"You're right, Jackknife," Robbie said. "But Andrés, Rufus's mole at the Good Hotel Barcelona, told us this morning that Ms. Günerro and her team headed to Madrid in the middle of the night. We're a half a day behind her, so it's better for us to figure it out while traveling."

"Actually, we can pinpoint where we're headed," Sophia said. "We just need to decipher the message Andrés intercepted the other day." She tapped a key on her laptop, and an image of a note appeared on the screen behind her. "Let's take a look."

> siba,
> I know of your troubles. i hope the west bengal silk housecoat i left for you makes you feel better. but you may have to sell everything you own.
> if you want to Remain president of the Good company, your payment to me and buNguu's too must now be "priceless."
> fortunately, U are in spain and there are plenty of priceless objects there. i have a troupe of Artists from everywhere— bangladesh, too—that "happily" stay at my castle in granada.
> you will comply. or Else.
> sincerely, ching Ching

A boy with black bed-head hair raised his hand. "Excuse me," he said. "Why is the formatting of this note so odd?"

"Good eye, Nicolas," Sophia said.

"They didn't even capitalize the proper nouns, like Bangladesh and Granada," Nicolas said. "There must be something up with that."

"There's clearly a hidden message here," Sophia said. "I need everyone in Tier Two looking into this. Nicolas and Sora, you two lead the search."

The computers on the side of the airplane lit up, and the kids dug in, searching for a clue. The kids clumped around Sora's and Nicolas's seats.

"For the rest of you," Robbie said, "Travis has a video he recorded this morning that he would like to share." Robbie pointed his index finger at Travis. "Let it roll."

"Okay, guys," Travis said, opening the computer in front of him. "This video is super scratchy because I had to copy it from a VHS tape."

"A what?" Terry asked.

"Don't worry about it," Travis said. "It's an old recording device, and this is some footage pulled from a BBC broadcast of a Southeast Asian newscast. Just watch."

Travis tapped a few keys on his computer, and the screen behind Robbie and Sophia lit up.

AN IN-FLIGHT MOVIE

The window shades hummed as they closed simultaneously and blocked the sun's glare. The image on the screen slowly came into focus. It was dark and gray.

The program then beeped three times.

All eyes in the airplane's boardroom locked on the screen.

The video was still hard to see, fuzzy, as if it had been taken by an old flip-phone camera. Travis tweaked his computer, and the TV program became brighter. On screen someone lifted a handwritten note that said, *This July on the border of Burma (Myanmar), and Bangladesh*.

Then the real video began. At first it was unfocused on a marsh with tall grass. A second later a man's voice whispered into a scratchy microphone.

"This is Daniel Foley, reporting for the New York Journal." He paused and adjusted the sound. "I am south of the financial city Chittagong at the Naaf River Wildlife Sanctuary. We are waiting here at the Bangladesh and Burma border for a glimpse of the secretive businessman known as Ching Ching. According to the Panama Papers, he is believed to be one of the richest men in Southeast Asia and reportedly trades in anything illegal."

The reporter pried the weeds back, and the camera showed a line of boys wrapped in yellow monk's gowns marching barefoot on a dirt road through the rain forest. The monks, all with clean-shaven heads, shouldered wooden artist easels.

Behind this group a man with a long white beard sat on a golden throne, which was strapped on two poles and carried by short men.

One by one, the boys in the yellow gowns walked across a metal plank with roped handrails and boarded a superyacht. The name on the bow read *Thimblerig*.

Daniel Foley reported again. "There are many aid agencies here helping stateless people. My sources tell me that these boys have lost their homes to wars and rising sea levels, and they have turned to this man for help."

The camera panned to the bearded gentleman on the throne and zoomed in.

"This is Ching Ching, who has kept these boys in a school here called Good Trade. But locals tell me Ching Ching doesn't teach anything; he has the boys in factories making counterfeit money, art, even basketball shoes. I've learned that he's putting these particular boys on the *Thimblerig*, a superyacht that is headed to Spain, where the children will be studying at the Good Art Institute of Granada."

The procession suddenly stopped, and the reporter paused.

"Tell them!" Ching Ching yelled from his throne. "Tell Bunguu and the woman he works with that the only payment I'll accept must be priceless or they will get none of my cash."

Ching Ching wafted his face with a fan made of five-hundred-euro bills.

The reporter whispered, "Ching Ching is referring to Lu Bunguu, supposedly one of Africa's wealthiest men and a notorious warlord. The woman he works with is anyone's guess."

The video stopped abruptly and cut to black.

CHAPTER 25

MONEY IS BEHIND EVERYTHING

Sophia adjusted the dimmer, and the lights grew brighter in the boardroom.

Robbie said, "I think we all know who this woman Ching Ching is referring to in the video."

"This is terrible," Kerala said. "This is another group of kids being forced to work for the Good Company. They might even be brainwashed into being Curukians."

"I agree," Astrid said. "We should be going to Granada. Not Madrid."

"None of this makes sense to me," Alister said. "Art. Weapons. Spain. Günerro?"

The airplane shook in a bubble of turbulence, and Sophia grabbed hold of the table as she stood.

"Let me connect the dots for you, as I now see it," she said, addressing the group.

Everyone sat back and listened.

"We know the Good Company is on the verge of bankruptcy," she said.

"That would be good news for us," said a girl in Tier Two.

"Ms. Günerro lost money," Sophia said, "on the failed kidnapping in Paris. Then she tried to get the

Kapriss diamonds. Again, failure. Enter Ching Ching. A person to whom Ms. Günerro and the Good Company owe a lot of money."

"In fact," Robbie said, "Mr. Benes, Coach Creed, and Rufus Chapman are upstairs in a meeting trying to figure out how they can buy parts of the Good Company if it goes bankrupt."

"That means," Alister said, "if Ms. Günerro is out of money, she'll have to sell everything—cars, houses, boats—just so she can pay her bills."

"Sorry," said a boy in Tier Two. "I'm still lost."

"Stay with us," Sophia said. "Ching Ching sells guns, actually weapons of all kinds. Dirty bombs. Mines. Anything that kills."

"So how does art fit in?" Kerala asked.

Robbie stood next to Sophia. "Art is sometimes used as currency—money," he said. "Art is something of value that bad guys use to trade with, and it's fairly easy to transport, too."

Sophia added, "Currently, there are more than a thousand Picassos that are reported stolen or missing." She paused for effect. "Art theft is a multibillion-dollar business, which is used to pay for other illegal activities."

"Such as . . ." said a girl from Tier Two.

Sophia glanced at Robbie.

"Money is behind everything," he said. "Good and bad."

"Typical!" said Astrid. "Siba Günerro and the Good

Company have figured a way to make money from just about everything bad in the world."

"So the painting is like a trophy," said a girl in Tier Two. "It's a game."

"It could be," Robbie said.

"But wait," Nalini said. "If you're going to steal a painting and then resell it, why have children with easels come all the way to Spain?"

"Remember," Sophia said. "Art is valuable, but it can also be copied."

"Cheaters," Terry called out.

Travis said, "They could hold the painting for ransom and threaten to destroy it if the museum didn't pay them."

"Or," Jackknife said, "if you own one million-dollar painting and sell copies as originals, then . . ." He paused. "Then you could have hundreds of copies. A hundred million dollars for fakes!"

"Exactly," Robbie said.

"And," Alister said, "if the person who bought the painting found out it was a phony, no one would say anything because they would have traded the painting for something illegal . . . like guns."

"Or people," Lucas said.

"Well put," Robbie said.

There was a moment of silence as everyone seemed to understand the lengths to which the Good Company would go in order to cheat to make money.

"What kind of art do they steal?" Lucas asked.

"All kinds," Sophia said. "Paintings, statues, one-of-a-kind pieces." She paused and clicked a key on her computer, and a map of Spain appeared on the screen behind her. She zeroed in on the capital. "Which brings us to Madrid, where we are heading today."

"But why Madrid?" asked Alister. "Why Spain?"

"First," Robbie said, "there are several groups in Spain, like the Basque separatists, with whom Ms. Günerro could work seamlessly."

"My guess," Sophia said, "would be the Prado Museum in Madrid, which has one of the largest collection of paintings in the world."

"Let's see if Ching Ching's note gives us a clue," Robbie said. He pointed to Sora Kowa. "Sora? Any luck deciphering the note?"

"Yes," she said, tapping her keyboard. "I think we've got it!"

She hit a button, and Ching Ching's note reappeared on the main screen.

"Notice," she said, pointing with an electronic pen. "Ching Ching's letter has odd breaks in the lines and capital letters used randomly. And he uses the letter *U* to mean you. Not odd in a text but strange in a handwritten note."

Sora highlighted eight letters from the note: *I, R, G, N, U, A, E, C.*

"It's quite simple," she explained. "An anagram of these letters reveals only two words. *Urgencia*, which is Spanish for urgency or emergency—and the other word is the only piece of artwork mentioned in the letter: *Guernica*."

"*Guernica*," Sophia said, "is the most famous anti-war painting in the world."

Astrid added, "One of Pablo Picasso's greatest works, but also a symbol of peace."

"And," Alister said, "perfect irony for a guy like Ching Ching who makes money from guns and war."

A girl with red pigtails sitting in Tier Two raised her hand. "I've got something else."

"Lily Hill," Robbie said. "Welcome to White Bird One. What's up?"

"I'm sure it's no coincidence that this is in today's *SpanArt Newspaper*," Lily said. She tapped a button on her computer, and an image of a tabloid paper appeared on the big screen.

The headlines were written in Spanish.

"Here's the English translation," she said, typing.

For a second, the robo-translator blurred the words, and then the title and text appeared in English. It read:

GALLERY THAT HOUSES GUERNICA AT THE REINA
SOFÍA TO GET COMPLETE OVERHAUL. PAINTING IS
BEING MOVED TODAY.

"The irony," Sophia said. "People who make money from war stealing an antiwar painting."

Robbie said, "Sounds like we've caught up with the Good Company."

The captain's voice came over the PA system. "Initial descent into Madrid. Please buckle up."

MADRID

The main cabin door opened, and Rufus Chapman peered out, the tails of his tuxedo flapping in the wind. He waved to the ground crew below, and a stair car puttered up to the plane.

The line of New Resistance kids followed Coach Creed, Rufus Chapman, and John Benes as they clomped down the steps and into an air-conditioned bus.

The Eurolines tour bus powered down the E-90 highway heading into the Spanish capital. Lucas stared out the window, his reflection and the landscape outside blurring in the glare.

Lucas dozed in and out.

As the traffic thickened, the bus slowed. The adults began strolling the aisle, checking in with the kids.

Mr. Benes tapped Lucas. "What's up with you?"

"A little nervous," Lucas said. "I guess."

Astrid leaned across the aisle and cut in. "I understand what he's saying," she said. "We're all anxious."

From the very center of the bus Coach Creed raised his voice and spoke to everyone. "Yeah," he said, "everybody's a little afraid. I got one thing to say to you all: Welcome to life, people."

"Well you know," Nalini said. "This is not exactly our life here."

"What do you mean by that?" Coach Creed asked. He didn't wait for an answer. Instead he stayed in "coach" mode. "This *is* your life, Nalini." He looked around as if to speak to the whole bus. "All of you. For the most part your lives right now consist of working to make the world a better place. Sure, what you do is dangerous and pretty scary stuff, but I would bet a lot of kids around the world would like to have the adventures you're having."

"I think Nalini's point," Astrid said, "is that someone else could be doing this for us, finding Ms. Günerro and her people."

"It's true," Nalini said. "We always have to go it alone."

"May I?" Rufus asked.

"Go ahead," Mr. Benes said.

"Speaking as a butler, as a person who has been in service his entire life, I say to you this," he said, his words deliberate. "If not you, then who?" He paused. "If not now, when?"

Everyone was quiet for a second.

A voice from the back of the bus called out. "Why not grown-ups?"

"The strength of the New Resistance," Mr. Benes said, "is that most people think kids are weak, so the perception of your abilities as children is underestimated. This perception is actually a strength that you can use to your advantage."

Astrid folded her arms and argued with her dad. "Being nervous is also a disadvantage. Maybe we need a break."

Coach Creed stepped between Lucas's and Astrid's seats. He didn't acknowledge Astrid's comment. He paused and looked at the group like a coach in a locker room at halftime.

"The other half of nervous is excited," Coach Creed said. "It's all a matter of how you look at things. You kids are much more capable than you think. Sure your brains are telling you that you can't, but you have to fight off this critic in your mind. You can always do more. You can always do more homework; you can always play another half, another quarter, another set. You can study harder, run for longer, and you can always leave things better than you found them."

Lucas knew Coach was right. He and the other kids *could* do more.

"You have it in you," Coach continued. "All of you. The next time you think about quitting or needing a break, know this fact: Your tank is still more than half full."

No one said anything. In a short while the traffic came to a standstill and the bus stopped. Nothing was moving. Mr. Benes talked to the driver.

A second later he came back and spoke to the kids. "There's construction blocking the road up ahead. We're as close as we can get."

"Let's go, people," Coach Creed said.

Terry Hines asked, "Are you coming with us to the museum, Coach?"

"I am," he said.

"Tier One is going with Chapman," Mr. Benes said. "And Coach Creed and I will each be taking a group."

"Yay!" said someone up front. "A field trip!"

"Yes," Rufus said, "we'll be your tour guides."

Everyone got off the bus and huddled together near the entrance to El Retiro Park.

As they prepared to leave, Mr. Benes said, "Everything's going to be just fine. Okay?"

"Oh sure," Jackknife said. "We're all going to the Reina Sofía Museum to see Ms. Günerro and her Good Company steal some art. What could possibly go wrong?"

CHAPTER 27

FIELD TRIP

Madrid's famous El Retiro Park was supposed to be a quiet retreat. For Lucas and the New Resistance it was unfortunately the calm before the storm.

The kids split into groups, and they took off down a tree-lined gravel pathway leading into the park. They passed the statues of kings and queens and Montezuma, and an odd white statue of real kids.

Sitting on a pedestal, completely still, were three live children. Two were Flamenco dancers, and one was a boy playing an air guitar. The kids changed positions and then froze again.

The park was packed. Everywhere pigeons and pedestrians, horses and cats, bikes and strollers, competed for space.

A band rattling on snare drums circled a pond. There were rowboats, sunbathers, and some girls fishing.

On the walkway in front of the water, skaters weaved in and out of a row of African men and women playing bongo drums. There were mimes screaming silently, a puppet show of Don Quixote on his horse, and a man moonwalking to Michael Jackson music blaring from a boom box.

Coach Creed moved fast and everyone kept pace.

They walked past the Crystal Palace, an iron-and-glass house whose prism windows cast rainbows on the surrounding pond.

Coach didn't let up. They circled through a rose garden in full bloom where the air smelled like perfume.

The three groups of New Resistance kids and their grown-up tour guides exited the park.

Tables and booths crammed the sidewalk. There were shoppers looking at books, magazines, and comics. There was a section of CDs and old record albums stacked against the trees. Two classical guitarists played an Andrés Segovia song.

The New Resistance didn't stop. They were on a mission. Lucas fell back from the group to look over a wall and down into the railway yard. A maze of electrical wires over a series of train tracks merged into the covered station. Some of the trains were moving. Others sat idle on the tracks.

Something caught Lucas's attention.

From behind a grassy knoll nearly hidden on the other side of this network of tracks, workers in bright yellow Day-Glo vests were painting what appeared to be abandoned shipping containers on train cars.

The freshly stenciled sign on the exterior read in English: WE MAKE THE GOOD THINGS IN LIFE . . . BETTER.

Lucas knew that only one company in the world would say something like that.

They were close.

CHAPTER 28

GUERNICA

Coach Creed, Mr. Benes, and Rufus Chapman led the three groups past the Atocha train station. In the sky above the surrounding buildings, huge construction cranes groaned, and the air smelled of fried chicken.

"Hey look," Jackknife said. "There's Kentucky Fried Chicken right there across the street. Let's eat!"

Nalini looked at him. "I told you you had worms."

"After the museum tour," Astrid said in her mom voice.

The group crossed a busy street and tunneled under a tower of scaffolding that surrounded the museum. The tourist crowds grew thicker. Lucas could pick out a dozen different languages around him as they moved closer to the Reina Sofía.

Like watchful eyes, two modern glass elevators rose on the exterior of the grand museum. Near the entrance, men sold T-shirts and scarves printed with artwork. In the plaza, workers in Day-Glo-yellow jackets were sweeping and picking up trash.

Lucas remarked. "I just saw some guys dressed like that at the train station."

"They're street cleaners, Lucas," Astrid said. "No big deal."

"I'm with you, Lucas," Travis said. "There *are* a lot of bright yellow jackets here. Too many to be a coincidence."

As they funneled into the museum, Lucas looked back. The Day-Glo cleaners swept, pushed trash-can carts, and picked up dog poop. To Lucas they looked like electric bugs scrambling from spot to spot.

Each New Resistance group queued up in a different line. Tier One crammed into a glass elevator and rode up to the second floor with Rufus Chapman. Lucas looked out the window onto the plaza below, where a group of Day-Glo cleaners were affixing bright yellow masks over their faces.

Before he could get a closer look, the bell on the elevator dinged.

Tourists moved in clumps and crowded the hallways. A docent with bleached-blond hair spoke to her group.

"In addition to many of Picasso's paintings," she said, walking backward, "the Reina Sofía is home to Miró's *Woman and Bird at Night*, Salvador Dalí's *The Persistence of Memory*, and Solana's *Procession of Death*."

The words gave Lucas a bad feeling. He spun around and looked for the other kids from the Globe Hotel. Aside from the Tier One kids, Lucas didn't see any of the rest. They were nowhere to be found.

"Should we wait on the others?" Kerala asked.

"We're all heading to the same spot," said Rufus,

"exactly where Ms. Günerro and *Guernica* are."

At the far end of a long corridor lined with statues, tourists clogged the entranceway to the famous *Guernica* room.

They hadn't been waiting ten seconds when they heard the voice.

"Rufus!" a woman called out.

Rufus and the Tier One kids in his group turned at the same time.

Ms. Günerro stood on her tippy toes at the entrance to the *Guernica* room and waved her hand high in the air above the heads of the waiting crowd.

Rufus looked at his group. "Boys and girls," he said. "It's showtime."

A guard in a green jacket came out, cutting a pathway. Rufus, along with Lucas, Astrid, Jackknife, Travis, Kerala, Nalini, and Alister, moved toward Ms. Günerro.

The CEO of the Good Company was dressed like a queen in a long black dress with a white sash and a diamond tiara perched above her cat-eye glasses.

"Rufus Chapman!" said Ms. Günerro with a devilish grin. "Are you leading a tour group today?"

"Hello, Ms. Günerro," Rufus said with clenched teeth. "How do you do?"

"Ah, Rufus," Ms. Günerro said. "I see you have the Benes Globe Hotel children with you. How wonderful!"

"You know them?" Rufus asked.

"We go way back," Ms. Günerro said, aiming her

eyes at Lucas and Astrid. "Yes, Lucy and Asterix and I are old friends."

No one corrected her, but Astrid asked Rufus, "How do you know Ms. Günerro?"

Rufus said, "I used to work at the Good Hotel in London."

"Water under the bridge," Ms. Günerro said. She looked back into the *Guernica* room. "Why don't you all come with me? I have a special pass to see the exhibit today. We'll be the last to see it before it's moved to its new home."

Lucas looked around the hallway to see if there were any more Day-Glo cleaners. He knew they had to be part of this puzzle. But there were none around, which worried him even more.

Kerala and Alister peered into the *Guernica* room. Another wave of museumgoers was just leaving through the doorway on the other side.

"Why do you have a special pass?" Astrid asked.

"Because," Ms. Günerro said. "*Guernica* is named after my family. Many years ago an immigration official misspelled Guernica and wrote Günerro instead, so my father's friend Pablo Picasso painted *Guernica* for the family."

Astrid's eyes bulged, and her mouth dropped open. She seemed at a loss for words.

"No he didn't," Travis said, snapping the silence. "Picasso painted it because Franco, the Spanish dictator, let Hitler bomb Franco's enemies in the Basque region.

Everyone was furious for the destruction it caused because the town of Guernica was a farming area and there were no soldiers, no army. Nothing military."

"That's why," Nalini said, adding to the argument, "there are farm animals and babies and mothers in the painting."

Kerala added. "It had nothing to do with you or your family."

"Well, well, well," Ms. Günerro said. "You do know that art is subjective. I just so happen to have a different interpretation."

Lucas scanned the crowd again. Coach Creed, Mr. Benes, and the other New Resistance tour groups had still not caught up.

A guard inside the *Guernica* room signaled Ms. Günerro, and Rufus and the Tier One kids followed.

They caught their first glimpse of the famous painting. For Lucas it was amazing to be so close to one of the greatest paintings ever. To see it online was one thing, but to see it in person, to be so close to it you could touch it, was something else.

The painting was colossal, taking up one entire side of the room.

Ghosts floated across a black, white, and gray canvas crowded with moaning mothers and dead animals. A wounded man. A terrified horse. A burning house. Everywhere, death.

A tour guide in a tan dress explained the painting to her group.

"*Guernica* is . . ." she said, pausing while the line broke apart and circled around to hear the story. "Picasso's *Guernica* is considered to be the art world's greatest condemnation of war."

For Lucas, seeing the mural-sized painting and hearing the tour guide made the story all the more real. For a brief moment he forgot about Ms. Günerro and her Good Company. Lucas stared at the painting and listened to the docent.

The woman cleared her throat and spoke in a monotonous tone. "The bombing was used to test newly invented bombs. So in effect, two dictators joined forces and killed innocent people and their farm animals for no reason."

There was a pause as the tourists leaned in to inspect the details in the painting.

Ms. Günerro cocked her head and spoke to Rufus as if they were best friends.

"Of course they tested the bombs," she said. She chuckled indignantly. "This is the world of business. You have to test your products, and your products have to work. If your bombs don't blow up, then no one will buy your bombs."

Lucas could feel that something wasn't right, and it wasn't just Ms. Günerro's idiotic speech about bombs blowing up. He spun around 360 degrees to take in his surroundings.

Picasso's early sketches of the famous painting hung on the opposite walls. Two guards in the corner napped in odd-looking metal chairs. And Ms. Günerro was now digging in her purse.

The New Resistance kids huddled.

"She's putting something in her ears," Nalini said.

"What is it?" Alister asked.

"I don't know," Kerala said.

"Earplugs," Astrid said.

Travis added. "That's what it looks like to me."

"Earplugs?" Jackknife asked.

Then it happened.

Fast.

A loud boom shook the building. Like an earthquake. No one knew what was going on.

On the opposite side of the room, ten Curukian girls wearing Day-Glo-yellow jackets and masks stormed the room.

A nightmare in the middle of the day had begun.

HEIST

In many high-stakes heists there's often a computer guy who hacks into the security system to disable it. Then of course there are cat burglars who rappel down through the air-conditioning vents and hang upside down to steal paintings deep in the dark of night.

Siba Günerro and the Good Company liked to do things their own way.

Another boom shook the museum. People screamed. From the other side of the room a dozen more Curukian girls charged in, toting jackhammers over their shoulders.

The two "napping" guards rose and somehow converted their chairs into stepladders. Then they mysteriously left the room.

The girls with jackhammers locked arms and pushed the crowd against a wall.

Bleach shouted in English, as if it were an Old West bank robbery, "On the floor!"

With a collective gasp everyone dropped to the ground. Like the others Lucas lay on his stomach. His friends huddled around, and Lucas lifted his head and looked over Astrid's back and watched.

Rufus had gotten separated and now was crouched in a corner with a group of Curukian girls standing guard over him. On the opposite side of *Guernica* Ms. Günerro sat in a chair. One of the Curukian girls handed her a thick wool blanket.

Lucas kept scanning the room, looking for a weak link. He hoped they would make a mistake and he could use it to his advantage. But he also knew that he had to be careful—these girls were deadly.

Whimpers and prayers in different languages began to fill the room as it seemed everyone was getting nervous. A woman on the other side of the room knelt and then fainted. Several women clutched their purses and hid them under their bodies. Mothers and fathers covered their children with their arms to protect them.

Little kids cried. Husbands and wives hugged. Old ladies and old men crouched on the floor in tight balls of horror. A man in the center of the room stood and clenched his fists and yelled at the girls in Spanish. He spoke so fast Lucas couldn't understand him. Then a Curukian girl jabbed him in the ribs with the handle of her jackhammer, and the man fell to the floor.

After this incident, the room fell into an eerie silence.

An alarm cut through the calm.

Three groups of new Curukian girls ran into the room carrying Miró's *Woman and Bird at Night*, Salvador Dalí's *The Persistence of Memory*, and

Solana's *Procession of Death.*

Then a horn blared throughout the museum.

Arrrr! Arrrr!

Deep and deafening.

Strobe lights above the entryway to the room flashed, making it difficult to see. A metal security gate clanged down from the ceiling, barricading the room and imprisoning the Curukians even before they had finished the job.

Thoughts raced through Lucas's mind. *Why did the thieves trap themselves? How will they get out? Hostages?*

The Curukian girls were fast. Ten jackhammers began to rattle on the wall around the *Guernica* painting. For a second, it sounded like phony gunfire.

Brrrat. Brrrat.

The people in the room covered their ears.

The thieves worked quickly, moving up and down and around the painting. The wall surrounding *Guernica* began to crumble. Fragments of plaster and stone rained down and scattered on the floor.

Behind him, Lucas heard more noise. He and Jackknife flipped over onto their backs.

Bleach and another group of girls had started jackhammering the exterior wall.

Bits and pieces of brick and concrete broke off and sprayed into the room.

From both sides of the room tiny particles of wall were exploding, and dust was filling the room with a gritty mist. Coughs competed with the unnerving clatter of jackhammers.

Lucas spotted the red light on the security camera blinking. The light sensors fired infrared lasers through the fog to get a reading. It was too thick. The cameras could see nothing; they could record nothing.

White dust and black noise filled the air of the *Guernica* room. The alarm continued to screech and beep.

Arrrr! Arrrr!

Some of the children started getting up, screaming while holding their ears, until their parents pulled them back down to the ground to safety.

Lucas had to do something. Like a soldier crawling through a marsh he snaked around the room toward Ms. Günerro. He worked his way through the deep powder on the floor, his feet scraping two long tracks behind him. Lucas spat, trying to keep from swallowing the powdery grit that was caking his lips.

Suddenly a blue light shot through the thick fog, followed by a shriek. One of the Curukian girls had hit an electrical wire, and the lights in the room shorted out. For a second, the girl wavered on the stepladder; then with a bang she dropped her jackhammer and fell to the floor, moaning.

The only light now in the room came from the bank of windows near the ceiling. The slanting rays cut through the glass, highlighting the dust in the air, making it even more difficult to see. The jackhammering began again as the Curukian crooks hurried their pace.

Lucas worked his way into the heart of the tourists who lay scattered and scared on the floor. He cleared his eyes and briefly could see Ms. Günerro crouching behind a chair, a blanket covering everything but her cat-eye glasses.

Armed with a jackhammer, Bleach stepped back as an entire section of the exterior wall tore free and fell into the street behind the museum.

The jackhammers stopped, and the dust began to settle.

Bleach and her girls had blasted the wall to smithereens and created a hole.

Brilliant, Lucas thought. *An escape route where one didn't exist before.*

Another section of brick and concrete fell to the outside, and a breeze blew into the room, scattering even more chalky powder.

Just outside this new hole in the wall, the last leg in the getaway was clear. The construction scaffolding that surrounded the museum provided the perfect escape route.

As police officers banged on the other side of the locked metal security gates, some of the tourists got up and tried to open the gate for them.

While there was still thick fog in the room Ms. Günerro stood and tossed her dust-covered blanket to the ground. She stepped through the opening in the wall and down the scaffolding and out of sight.

Bleach and the Curukian girls followed, carrying *Guernica* and the other paintings down the ramp. They left the girl who had been shocked behind.

Lucas hopped up and looked down into the street. There were six waiting construction trucks that looked exactly alike. He watched the girls lay the paintings in the back of only one truck.

All six trucks sped away in six different directions.

In a matter of minutes, several priceless paintings and the most famous antiwar painting in the world, Pablo Picasso's *Guernica*, were gone.

DUST TO DUST

The dust began to settle.

Chatter filled the room as the witnesses to the theft unglued themselves from the floor. They looked like they had been bombed with bags of flour. They brushed the fine powder from their clothes and looked around. A group of men tried to unlock the barricaded doors.

Lucas and the Tier One kids gathered by the giant hole in the wall. Rufus Chapman dusted himself off and joined the kids.

"We knew exactly what was going to happen," Rufus said. "But not how."

"The question remains," Nalini said. "What are we going to do now?"

For a second, no one answered. A warm breeze blew into the room formerly known as the *Guernica* room.

"We don't do anything right now," Astrid said.

Travis wiped his face. "Should we wait for the police?"

"No one will believe a bunch of kids," Kerala said.

"Kerala's right," Jackknife said. "No one would ever believe a rich person like Ms. Günerro would steal."

CHAPTER THIRTY

"We have to do something," Nalini said, brushing dust from her skirt.

"It's going to take some time," Alister said, "for them to unlock those gates. They're on special timers."

"We don't have time," Jackknife said.

Outside the museum, police and ambulance sirens wailed. Deep in his gut Lucas could feel what was right.

He shook his head. "If we wait around here," he said, "the cops will come in and detain us and ask us questions for hours."

"While Ms. Günerro gets away with the paintings," Rufus said.

"Exactly," Lucas said.

"We'll be here all afternoon," Nalini said.

"But that's what you're supposed to do," said Astrid, "in this situation. We know who did it. We have proof."

Lucas suppressed his anger. "I know it's what you're supposed to do," he said. "But this seems like one of those times that we should do what is best for this situation and not necessarily what is supposedly right."

Lucas wasn't finished. "And," he continued, "we're the only ones who know for a fact who stole the paintings, *and* we know where they went."

"We don't know where Ms. Günerro took the paintings," Astrid said.

Rufus folded his arms. "Seems Lucas may have an idea."

"All we know," Nalini added, "is that they went through this hole in the wall and down into the street and into the backs of some trucks."

"That is true," Alister said.

"Except," Lucas said, "I saw the same Day-Glo-yellow jackets in the railway yard. Some guys were painting shipping containers. And I know they belong to the Good Company."

"How do you know," Astrid asked, "that they belong to the Good Company?"

Lucas said, "The painters' sign said 'We Make the Good Things in Life . . . Better.'"

Everyone nodded.

"Sounds like our friends at the Good Company," Jackknife said.

"What about the others in our group?" Nalini asked.

"Don't worry," Rufus said. "I'll get them."

Rufus grabbed Lucas's arm. "Before you go," he said. "Your father and Coach Creed and I will track you as best we can. We'll get word to you so you'll know where to find to us."

"How will we know?" Jackknife asked.

"The message will be obvious to you," Rufus said.

"Map Boy," Astrid said. "Lead the way."

CHAPTER 31

SUBWAY SURFERS

News and police helicopters thundered in the sky above the museum. The air still smelled of chalky concrete powder. And the kids of the New Resistance readied themselves for the next part of the mission.

Lucas felt a burst of freedom as his mind mapped the way. He stepped through the hole in the wall and onto the scaffolding. Using the crossbars, he flipped down to the next level, where he landed on dusty boards. From there he jumped onto the sidewalk.

People were running in all directions. No one seemed to know what had just happened.

Behind him Lucas could sense that his friends were following.

The group of kids wound its way down an old cobblestone street, past the KFC, and across a busy intersection. It seemed they were now going in the opposite direction, as everyone else was rushing to the robbery at the Reina Sofía. They cut through the waiting taxicabs and past an old woman with a white face playing with kittens.

Lucas thought for a second it was Siba Günerro in disguise.

The kids moved to go inside the Atocha train

station. They darted through the tropical garden filled with exotic plants and palm trees that scraped the atrium's glass ceiling. They stopped for a second at the pond located at the end of the indoor forest. People were leaning over a railing and looking at hundreds of turtles swimming in the water and climbing up the bank.

The New Resistance kids snapped out of the turtle trance and met up underneath the train schedules.

"Where do you think Ms. Günerro's going?" asked Kerala.

"Granada," Travis said. "That's where the monk boys, the Burmese painters, on the *Thimblerig* were being taken."

"Supposedly," Astrid said.

"Travis is right," Jackknife said. "That's the only place she'd go at this point."

The schedule board said there were several trains leaving that afternoon, but they would have to change later in the day at another station.

"These schedules are only for passenger trains," Alister said.

"Ms. Günerro," Travis said, "would have her own train."

"You would think," Jackknife said.

"And there are no freight trains at this station," Nalini said.

"Which," Lucas said, "is exactly why it's weird that there are train cars with Good Company shipping containers on them in the railway yard."

"Those are probably intermodal," Travis said. "She could have them hooked to a train in no time."

"With the Good Company," Astrid said, "anything is possible."

Lucas looked at his friends and took off running through the station, and the others followed. He rushed out to an empty platform where a single silver train waited on a track. There was a lone luggage cart stacked with suitcases but no passengers.

Astrid put her hands on her hips. "We can't run out onto the tracks, Lucas."

"It's ridiculously dangerous," Travis added.

"And security's tight," Alister said. "This is the same station that terrorists bombed on March eleventh, 2004."

"Well then," Lucas said. "It looks like we'll have to do some subway surfing to get to the Good Company train cars."

Jackknife was already way ahead of him. He had taken a pile of travelers' luggage and stacked suitcases into a step formation.

The kids scrambled up the makeshift staircase and climbed on top of a train car. The train next to them slowly began to depart the station.

Without warning Jackknife jumped and landed on the moving train. Lucas and the others followed. Ducking under the electrical wires, they scrambled on the roof all the way down to the front car.

The train left the covered part of the station and crept into the railway yard. The sun was high overhead, and the metal rooftops began to sizzle.

From this vantage point, Lucas pointed out the Good Company train cars in the distance. A group of Curukians was closing a door on one of the containers, and a locomotive was backing up to the train.

In a few seconds' time the kids hopped to another train that was slowly entering the station. This time they scurried to the last car.

In the middle of the network of tracks a high-speed AVE train (known as *El Pato*—the Duck—because of its long beak) was sitting idle. The lights on the inside were off.

From the top of their slow moving train, the kids leaped onto the Duck's roof.

On the other side of the railway yard the Good Company locomotive backed up to the train of containers. A metal clang rang out as the cars connected.

"The Picasso train is leaving the station," Jackknife said. "All aboard."

The kids slid down the slanted nose of the Duck and sprinted across the maze of tracks. The Good Company train lurched forward and began heading out.

The Tier One kids were only one hundred meters, some 328 feet, away from the Good Company shipping containers.

They sprinted on the railway ties, chasing down the train.

Suddenly out of nowhere a horn blasted. Lucas looked up. Another train was coming directly at them. The locomotive was slowing down, but Lucas and his friends were directly in line to get crushed.

The engineer flashed his lights and blew the horn again.

The kids leaped over to the next track just as the train thundered past.

They kept running. The Good Company train was now only twenty meters, sixty-five feet, away.

Jackknife sprinted and got to the train car first. He unclipped the lock and flung open the container door. In one move he flipped himself up into the metal box. Jackknife lay on the floor bracing his legs against a pair of hooks on the wall. The train sped up, and the kids ran faster after it. Jackknife stretched out his right arm, and one by one his friends climbed up into the container.

On the opposite end, an opening led to the other train cars. Sunlight flashed into the metal box that would soon be their temporary home. Kerala closed the back door that they had come through and latched it.

The boxcar was as hot as an oven.

The kids collapsed on the dusty floorboards. No one spoke. They were officially stowaways on a Good Company train.

BOXCAR CHILDREN

The train clicked and clacked along the tracks with a slow and methodical rhythm.

Lucas could feel the metal wheels below as they thumped faster and faster down the two iron rails. The locomotive left the capital city and increased its speed, dragging the Good Company container cars through graffitied suburbs and into the golden Spanish countryside.

Trapped inside this box, Lucas felt lost and needed some geographical orientation.

Tiny rays of light entered the container through bullet holes in the metal walls. For Lucas the openings provided miniature windows to the outside.

Fields and farms blinked by. Lucas stared at rows and rows of olive trees racing alongside the train. To him they looked like the long legs of a sprinter trying to keep pace.

For hours the train stayed mainly on the plains, passing windmills and whitewashed villages. Lucas looked at his friends crashed on the floor around him as the train clattered along.

Eventually Lucas gave in to sleep. His head rocked back and forth, and soon he settled in a corner and fell into a dream.

Deep in the dark, the nightmare that Lucas had had so many times before came to life.

Suddenly a banging sound pummeled through the container and woke everyone.

The door on the train car just in front of their container creaked open. A gust of cool wind rushed in, and the noise of the train clunking over the tracks rattled Lucas's mind.

Several people stepped in, their silhouettes blocking the light from the other car.

"Get up," Bleach said.

She led a team of girls to snatch the New Resistance kids and hauled them to the opening. A gap of maybe one meter, some three feet, separated their container from the next train car. Just below them the tracks clicked past in a blur.

Two Curukian girls stood in the next compartment holding the door open. The choice was simple. Either jump to the next train car and live or resist and get pushed to the tracks, where the iron wheels would pulverize them.

One by one Lucas and his friends hopped over the gap and into the next compartment.

From the outside, this container on a flatbed looked like any other. The metal exterior appeared to be dented, with peeling and chipped paint. But with the Good Company, things were not always as they seemed.

The inside of this car was far from being a simple shipping container. The New Resistance kids stepped into a full-blown, luxurious, private apartment-on-a-train. It looked like it belonged to a queen. Red mahogany wood paneling covered the walls. Persian rugs spread across the floor. At the far end, still wearing her tiara and perched in an ornate thronelike chair, was Siba Günerro.

"Welcome," she said, opening her arms. "Please join me."

The Curukian girls forced the New Resistance kids to sit on the rug at Ms. Günerro's feet. Lucas flashed back to kindergarten reading time.

Bleach and her Curukian clique left the room. Wearing brand-new security uniforms, Ekki and Goper stepped in and stood guard at the front and back doorways.

"So glad you could visit me," Ms. Günerro said. "Together I think we have just witnessed quite possibly the greatest art heist, ever. Wouldn't you agree?"

"You're sick," Astrid spat.

Ms. Günerro was calm and confident. "It was beautifully executed, if you ask me. What more could you possibly want from a museum tour? It was terribly exciting."

"You're right," Nalini said. She nudged Jackknife and Astrid.

Lucas considered her tone. He realized Operation Obnoxious was in motion. They were going to confuse Ms. Günerro again by nettling her with questions and comments.

"True," Alister said. "Museum tours are the worst."

"Right you are, young man," said Ms. Günerro with a proud grin.

The New Resistance kids crowded around the CEO's feet.

"Excuse me, Ms. Günerro?" asked Jackknife in the nicest voice Lucas had ever heard him use. "How much do you think the *Guernica* painting cost anyway?"

"The question, young man," Ms. Günerro said, "is not how much does it cost but rather what is its value?"

"Please tell us," said Kerala. "What's it worth?"

"I would imagine a hundred million US dollars," said Ms. Günerro. "Maybe more."

"I disagree," Astrid said. "*Guernica* doesn't have a value, per se," she said as she leaned against the wall. "I would argue that the painting is priceless."

The kids grumbled in agreement.

"It is priceless," said Kerala.

"Art is not science," Travis said. "You can't measure art."

"Art and value are both subjective," said Nalini.

"I agree," said Ms. Günerro. "So long as you can determine the price."

"Truly," said Alister. "There's no value other than what we receive or perceive from a particular painting."

Lucas listened. He couldn't believe the baloney his

friends could come up with.

"No, no, no," said Ms. Günerro, stomping her foot. "You're all wrong. The value is how much someone will pay us for it—I mean pay a person for it."

"This is silly talk," Goper said. "They're trying to confuse the situation. I was a kid in middle school once. I know what they're doing. That's why Lucas is not talking."

"Yeah," Ekki said from the back of the car. "What he said."

Ms. Günerro turned toward Goper. "What do you think we should do then?"

"I think," Goper said, "that Lucas Beans is the real problem. The others are just brats."

"Very well, Goper," Ms. Günerro said calmly. "Take the math boy out of the equation and we'll have no more problems."

She chuckled.

"He might still have some secrets," Goper said.

"Goper, you're getting smarter by the day," Ms. Günerro said. "Yes, I do think I will make you head of Good Company Security—one day."

Goper smiled broadly.

"Why don't you and Ekki take Lucas to see the paintings," Ms. Günerro said, "while I get some more quality time with these kids."

Goper and Ekki lifted Lucas by the shoulders.

"And once he's seen the paintings," Ms. Günerro said, "tie him up with Ekki's little friend."

CHAPTER THIRTY-TWO

"Hircus?" Ekki asked.

"Yes," Ms. Günerro said. "That beast you insisted on carting around with us."

Goper and Ekki pushed and pulled Lucas through the gap between the train cars and into the next compartment.

This part of the train looked like a regular overnight passenger train, with sleeping bunks, bathrooms, and a café car. They continued to march through the moving train and cut through an equipment compartment with shovels, axes, and the jackhammers the Curukians had used to blast through the museum walls.

Goper pushed Lucas on, and they crossed into the next car.

Dangling from the ceiling, a single lightbulb swayed with the rocking of the train. A dull white shone on the paintings leaning against the wall.

Picasso's *Guernica* took up the whole left side, while on the right a fat yellow strap held the other stolen paintings against the wall.

Ekki and Goper marched Lucas between the artwork, down the center aisle covered in hay, and into the next train car.

Lucas cringed and covered his nose. This compartment stank. He gagged as he tried to pinpoint the odor.

Old wet basketball shoes, he thought. *Not quite. Maybe . . . vomit. No, not that, either. Dirty armpits.*

That's it.

Using a sisal rope, Ekki tied Lucas's wrists behind his back. Goper forced Lucas to the floor, and he lay in a pile of hay. Ekki looped Lucas's ankles together and then lashed the ropes to a hook of some kind on the wall.

Below the sheet metal floor the train thundered across the tracks.

Lucas could barely move, and he felt particularly vulnerable because he couldn't see a thing. And he was dying to know what was making that awful smell.

"Hey," Lucas asked, "can you guys turn on a light?"

"There's no light in this room," Goper said.

Ekki rattled a tiny box. "I have some matches," he said.

"Smoking is stupid," Goper said. "Everybody knows that."

"Well, did you know—" Ekki said.

"Yes," Lucas said, frustrated with their banter. "Did you know there is hay in this car, and this whole train will catch on fire if you strike a match in here?"

"Oh," Ekki said. "Good point."

Goper slapped his partner. "Let's go."

The guards turned to leave.

"Wait," Lucas asked. "What's that smell?"

"Oh," Goper said. "That's your new roommate, Hircus."

CHAPTER 33

THE TRAIN STAYS MAINLY ON THE PLAIN

Lucas found himself tied to a wall inside a dark train car that stank like armpits. He yanked on the cords and twisted his fingers to untangle the knots, but it only made the ropes tighter.

The purpose of a knot or hitch was to hold something until you wanted to untie it. Unfortunately, the clump Ekki had put together was not a knot. It was some haywire jumble of fibers. Lucas tugged on the ropes again, but he knew it would be impossible to undo. He would have to figure out something else.

He buried his head in a pile of hay and drifted into thought.

He tried his best to avoid thinking about his current situation.

Sometimes when you're alone, you can figure out who you are or who you want to be. Spend a little time alone, and your heart and your mind will connect and let you know what you should do.

This was not exactly what Lucas had envisioned as a good time to think about what was important in life. A camping trip would have been better. Lucas couldn't help but think about all the kids who he had seen and met who were not free to do as he was. But now he wasn't free either. He was a good guy and he was going to do some good in the world. That much he knew.

His mind wandered back to the beginning. This mission had started with his mother's cryptic message.

Priceless, he thought. *What is more valuable than priceless?*

He nodded as he felt his heart speaking clearly to him. He could *feel* the answer coming. He rolled over and lay in the hay and listened.

He soon heard a noise. A rustling. Someone was in the compartment with him. Lucas's whole body tensed with fear.

"Hello?" he called out cautiously.

"Hello?" he said again.

Something deliberate moved in the hay. Footsteps. Lucas counted but it was dark in the compartment, and he couldn't tell if it was two feet or four.

Then he heard "Baa."

Lucas got up on his knees and his eyes adjusted.

"Baa," said the voice.

Lucas stretched his neck and looked deep into the dark compartment. He was face-to-face with a goat.

A goat? Lucas thought. *Hircus is a goat?*

He was most definitely a goat, a stinky one. But Hircus also gave Lucas an idea.

The solution to many problems is often very close at hand. Or in this case: *very close at mouth.*

In the dark Lucas looked in the direction of the

goat. "You must be Hircus," he said.

"Baa," the goat bleated.

"You're probably hungry. Aren't you?"

"Baa."

"I bet you'd like some yummy rope for a midnight meal!"

Lucas turned around and backed up to the goat and offered the knot as a snack. At first Hircus licked the salt from Lucas's palms.

"Go ahead," Lucas said. "You can have the whole thing."

The goat crunched on the knot, and Lucas curled his fingers, hoping Hircus was a vegetarian like the Curukian girls.

For a few minutes the goat munched and chomped on the rope like it was the best meal he'd ever had.

About halfway through the goat's dinner the clunking of the train wheels grew deeper and seemed to be slowing. Lucas knew that if the train stopped he would have only a few minutes to escape. He looked back over his shoulder.

"There's a lot of fiber in rope," Lucas said. "It's just like cereal. It's good for you, Hircus. Keep on eating."

The old goat seemed to understand. He chomped down one more time on the knot, and Lucas felt the jumble loosen just enough. He wiggled his wrists and slid his hands free; then he untied the ropes from his ankles.

Soon the train slowed to a crawl.

Lucas petted Hircus on the head. "It's time for me to go," he said. "And I think you might want to brush your teeth before bed!"

Lucas wiped the goat slobber from his hands. Then he bent down and grabbed a loose metal plank in the floor and ripped it clean off.

He stared down through the gaping hole in the container and watched the railroad ties click past. He listened for the slowing rhythm. In a few moments the metal wheels squeaked as the train braked.

Lucas would not have much time to escape. He lowered himself onto the railcar frame; just below him the tracks rolled by. If he slipped, he would be sliced into thirds.

He waved good-bye to Hircus and slid the flooring back over the hole he had created. Then he held on for dear life.

The train finally came to a complete stop, and a long whistle sang out. As far as Lucas could tell, they were still in the countryside.

On both sides of the tracks he spotted boots running toward the back of the train. Ekki and Goper, Lucas figured.

Someone's walkie-talkie screeched in Spanish, "Waiting for another train to clear the route."

In the distance Lucas could hear the rumble of a passing train. The boots ran past again, and Lucas eased himself down onto the railroad ties, between the rails. Above him, he stared at the bottom of the train car. For a second he felt claustrophobic.

Lucas crossed his arms over his chest and lay perfectly still. As he waited, he could feel the pressure building in every cell in his body.

Three minutes later, a whistle wailed into the night. The train lurched forward, and the metal couplings connecting the cars clanged together.

Lucas had to move. In just a second the train would travel over him. He knew he wouldn't be able to handle that. And there were chains hanging underneath the car that would shred him like cheese.

The space between the front wheels of the car and the back wheels provided plenty of room, if he was fast enough. Before the train really started moving, he had to bolt.

As the train horn blasted, Lucas let out the scream that had been brewing in his gut.

In one motion Lucas rolled over the rail between the moving wheels of the train and into a rock bed. The train kicked in and started moving down the tracks.

Click. Clack.

REFUGE

The red lights at the back of the train faded into the darkness, leaving Lucas all alone in the middle of nowhere.

For a good long while he waited and lay still in the grass that ran alongside the railroad tracks. He wanted to make sure the train was truly gone and that no one had seen him.

Briefly he replayed in his mind what had just happened. He had rolled between moving train wheels.

He thought, *Don't try this at home, kids.* He laughed at being able to make fun of something that had been so scary.

The joke got him going, and he collected his thoughts. Lucas hopped up and started walking along the tracks with no real destination in mind. He knew somehow, someway he had to get to Granada, where his friends and the stolen artwork would soon be. He figured he was several hours away on foot.

So he just started putting one foot in front of the other. It was the only way to get anywhere.

A waning crescent moon drifted over the land.

The light made the train tracks glisten as if they

had been oiled. Lucas followed the two iron rails for about half an hour. Soon he felt himself moving slower and slower. He would have to rest.

In about four kilometers, roughly two and a half miles, he spotted the tiny light of a farmhouse in the middle of what looked like a vineyard.

Lucas left the tracks and scrambled through the underbrush and down into a field. He cut between two rows of vines. They were laden with thick bunches of grapes. Food and something to drink at the same time. He stuffed his face with the biggest, fattest red grapes he could find, the juice pouring between his fingers and down his neck.

He couldn't believe how sweet they were.

He ate for a few minutes, and then pure exhaustion hit him. He guessed the time was about two-thirty in the morning, and he knew he had to stop. The choices out here were slim. He thought about curling up in the dirt under the vines and sleeping for a few hours, at least until sunrise.

On second thought, he would take his chances and check out the farmhouse and see if he could possibly sneak into the barn and catch a few winks.

He cut diagonally through the vineyard and came to the house. The white building was a circular structure with a conical thatched roof. Around the property there were no cars or bikes or motorcycles visible. A few pieces of farm equipment lay stacked in a pile. No way to get out quickly.

A distinct horse smell came from the attached barn.

Lucas peered through a small window in the main building. Inside he saw an old man in scruffy-looking clothes plucking feathers from doves.

Lucas could feel his brain shutting down. He had to do something quick. In the moonlight he scurried over to the barn and listened. No one. Still, he would have to be super quiet. He nudged his shoulder between the two doors and pried them open just a bit. He slipped his head inside. Soft moonlight shone through a window, and he could see horses in some of the stalls.

He stepped into the barn and discovered a perfect hideout. Lucas would crawl into a stall, and the old man would never know.

He creaked open a metal gate.

"Buenas noches," said a voice behind him.

Lucas's heart jumped into his throat.

The old man hit a switch, and a dim light illuminated the barn.

In Spanish Lucas said the same back to the man. "Good evening."

"May I help you?" the man asked in Spanish.

Lucas calculated that this guy was going to do him no harm at all. In fact he probably could even help Lucas.

They spoke Spanish.

"I'm lost," Lucas said.

"What are you doing out here in the dead of the

night by yourself?"

Again Lucas decided that honesty was the best policy.

"I'm sure you've heard about the art heist at the Reina Sofía yesterday," he said.

The man nodded.

"I was there when the robbery took place," Lucas said. "And I know who it was, and I have been tracking the stolen paintings all night."

"The police have no leads," the old man said. "But you're telling me that a lost boy in my barn knows who did it and where they are?"

Lucas nodded. "I don't lie about things that matter."

"Where do you think the paintings are?"

"They're on a train to Granada," Lucas said. "They're going to the Good Art Institute."

"How did you get here?"

"I was on the train," Lucas said. "But I hopped off."

"And then you ate my grapes."

Lucas swallowed. "Sorry," he said, wiping his cheek. "I was starving and thirsty."

The man glanced over at the horses in the stalls.

"You look tired," he said. "Come in and you can eat and drink and rest awhile."

The inside of the little cottage smelled of garlic, onions, and meat. The old man gestured for Lucas to take a seat at the wooden table in the center of the room.

In a moment the man put a deep bowl of pringa

meat stew and a clump of crunchy bread in front of him. Lucas devoured it almost without breathing.

When he was finished, Lucas took his plate to the sink where the old man was washing a few dishes.

"I don't sleep much," the old man said. "You can take my bed there in the corner."

"What are you going to do?"

"I am going to call a friend."

The man pointed Lucas toward a cot in the corner.

Lucas didn't argue. He crawled into the single bed while the man finished cleaning up.

"Buenas noches," said the man. "Good night."

Lucas didn't hear him. He was already fast asleep.

CHAPTER 35

THE ALHAMBRA

Somewhere in the wee hours of the morning before the sun rose, the Good Company train carrying the stolen paintings arrived at the Granada train station.

The train tracks terminated between two small concrete platforms. On one side, rows of locomotives sat idle. On the other, wooden benches lined a lobby covered in mosaic tiles.

Bleach and her Curukian girls unlocked the private sleeping compartments where Astrid, Jackknife, and the other New Resistance kids slept. The kids got up and shuffled to the café car. Wearing a housecoat and with her hair in curlers, Ms. Günerro sat alone at the far table drinking tea.

The kids didn't speak while they had bread and hot chocolate for breakfast. Astrid and Travis stared out the windows and watched.

A moving van backed up to the train. A sign on the side read:

VAN GOGH

ART MOVERS:

FINE ART TRANSPORTS LOCAL & INTERNATIONAL

Ekki and Goper supervised a team of Curukians toting paintings from the train to the waiting truck. Within a quarter of an hour the job was finished. Ekki locked the back doors, and the moving van rumbled away.

A few minutes later Bleach, Ekki, and Goper burst into the café car.

"Lucas is missing," Goper announced.

"Where did he go?" Ms. Günerro asked.

"We don't know," Bleach said.

Ekki said, "Hircus ate Lucas's ropes."

"If he jumped from the train," Bleach said. "Then he's probably—"

"Oh how dreadful," Ms. Günerro said. "That would be tragic."

"What if Lucas is still alive?" Goper said. "You know he's proven to be persistent."

"You're right, Goper," Ms. Günerro said. "Search the train one more time, and if you can't find him, then let's put our guests in the hotel basement with our artist friends."

Ekki, Goper, Bleach, and her clique scoured the train. When they came up empty-handed, they began lining up everyone to go to the hotel.

The city of Granada was mostly still asleep when the Good Company Security team marched the New Resistance kids through town. The sun hadn't risen yet, but the smell of fresh-baked bread drifted along the cobblestone streets.

Half an hour later the group crossed a tiny bridge and marched up a rock path to the back of the Alhambra.

A woman wearing a pilot's cap opened the gate for them.

"Buenos días," she said.

"Good morning," Goper said back in English. "We're going to the Good Art Institute of Granada."

"Yes," she said. "I heard."

The Alhambra was a former Moorish royal palace, a geometric fortress with a maze of courtyards and gardens filled with flowering bushes, cypress trees, and reflecting pools.

When they entered the gardens, the sun was just starting to rise. The bright yellow light sprinkled across the tops of the trees, and the birds sang.

Bleach and her Curukian girls didn't seem to care about the beauty of the place. Like mindless people, they did their jobs without thinking. They marched the remaining New Resistance kids—Astrid, Jackknife, Travis, Kerala, Nalini, and Alister—across the grounds, around a grove of young trees protected by green fencing, and to the hotel.

From there they descended the stairs to a cool and dark basement. Blue and yellow tiles covered the walls as they weaved deeper into a network of hallways. They passed through a door decorated in a white mosaic. Down a few more steps the walls turned into a maze of mirrors, and suddenly they were in a dark and dank corridor. As they marched down this hallway, the sound of their shoes clopping on the stone floor echoed.

Goper opened a wooden door leading into a cell. "Put them in here," he said.

Bleach asked, "What about the artist monks?"

"They're behind the gate in the next cell," Goper said. "Ekki and I will watch them both. You get back to the train with Ms. Günerro."

"But—" Bleach said.

"No buts," Goper said. "I am going to be head of Good Company Security. Soon. So you better get used to taking orders from me."

Bleach and her girls left.

Goper closed the door behind the New Resistance kids and locked them in the cell.

Alister raised his briefcase. "I can pick these locks," he whispered. "And look at this." He slid two barrel bolts on the door. "We can actually lock them out."

"We don't need to keep them out," Astrid said. "We need to get ourselves out."

The kids looked around the room. The jail had cots and bathrooms and a little kitchenette. It was like a hotel room with a connecting door to the next cell— except there was a gate with metal bars separating the two rooms.

A murmuring sound came from the other side.

The New Resistance team huddled in front of the gate and peered through the bars. The boys in yellow robes they had seen getting on the *Thimblerig* on the video were in a circle, meditating.

Travis put his face to the bars. "Psst," he said into the other room.

One of the boys rose and came to the gate. He had black hair and a round face. He smiled broadly.

"Hello," he said.

"Hi," Travis said. "You guys from Burma?"

"Yes," said the boy in English. "It's called Myanmar now."

"So you're the artists?" Travis asked.

"No."

"What do you mean?" Astrid asked. "You all have easels."

"And giant canvases," Kerala added.

"We are not creative artists," the boy said. "We have technique. We copy. Very fast. Very good."

"Sounds like an artist to me," Alister said, poking his head into the conversation.

Kerala asked. "Do you work for Ms. Günerro?"

"Yes, no," the boy said. "We are *forced* to work for her. It is not our choice."

"Let me get this straight," Travis said. "You're here to copy the stolen paintings. Right?"

The boy nodded. "We must or Ching Ching will make our families pay."

"Why don't you just escape?" Jackknife asked.

"Because," said the boy, "Ms. Günerro and Ching Ching would find us, and I don't want to think about what they would do."

Travis moved ahead with his questions. "How long does it take to copy a painting?"

"When we work together, we are much better."

"Travis?" Nalini asked. "Where are you going with all of this?"

Travis smiled. "Trust me," he said. "Getting the paintings copied is the key to getting out of here."

HUBRIS

Travis's idea didn't seem to make any sense to anyone. Astrid, Nalini, Jackknife, Alister, and Kerala stared at him.

"Getting the paintings copied," said Astrid, folding her arms, "will only keep us locked in here longer."

"It does seem," Nalini said, "a tad bit counterintuitive."

"That's the point," Travis said. "One thing we know about the Good Company is that you have to turn the tables on them."

"Every day," said Kerala, "is opposite day."

"Okay," Jackknife said. "What's this grand plan?"

"This idea will work perfectly with a little hubris," Travis said.

"What's that?" Jackknife asked. "Can you eat it like hummus?"

"Hubris," Travis said, "is too much pride or self-confidence."

Alister said, "Thinking you're better than everyone else."

"I know a lot of people like that," Nalini said.

"I still don't follow your plan," Astrid said.

"Watch this," Travis said.

A small window with tiny bars in the main door provided the only opening to the hallway. Ekki and Goper were sitting in plastic chairs, rocking on the back legs. Travis peered out and banged on the wooden door.

"Hey, Goper," he said.

"What do you want?"

"Do you really think you're going to be made head of Good Company Security?"

"I've got a pretty good feeling about it," Goper said. "Ms. Günerro sees my potential, and I know I'm *more* than perfect for the job."

"Well of course you are," Travis said. "But how long do you think you'll have to wait?"

"I shouldn't have to wait," Goper said. "Mr. Magnus has been arrested, and the spot for head of Good Company Security is officially wide open."

"My man Goper," Ekki said, "is number one!"

"If he's number one," Travis said, "the best of the best—"

"Yep," Ekki said.

"—then why," Travis asked, "hasn't Ms. Günerro given him the job already? What is she waiting for?"

Astrid seemed to pick up on Travis's game plan. She tippy-toed and spoke through the tiny window.

"What did Ms. Günerro just say to you on the train?" she asked. "I believe she said, quote, 'You're right, Goper.'"

"Yep," Ekki said. "I remember that!"

CHAPTER THIRTY-SIX

Jackknife joined in. "I heard Magnus waited decades for that position."

"Decades?" Goper said.

"Goper is not waiting no stinking decade," Ekki said. "That's like ten years."

"Of course he's not waiting," Astrid said.

Travis added, "You're more than qualified right now."

"You bet I am," Goper said.

The mop-headed Good Company guard leaned forward and dropped the front legs of his chair to the floor. Ekki did the same, and they both stared at the kids crowded around the cell-door window.

"Well," Travis said, "Astrid and I were just talking with these artists that you've brought over from Burma, and they said that they were inspired to paint."

"So," Ekki said.

"They're inspired right now," Astrid said, pushing her face into the tiny window.

"What do you mean 'right now'?" Goper asked. "They want to start working right after breakfast?"

Ekki said, "I like taking naps after breakfast."

Nalini nudged her way in. "You know," she said softly, "Picasso once said that inspiration exists, but it must first find you working."

"Well," Ekki said, "Picasso was one smart cookie."

"He was and so is Goper," Travis said, pausing for effect, "the next head of Good Company Security."

"I like the way that sounds," Goper said with an enormous grin.

"Me too," said Ekki.

"I've got an idea," Travis said. "If you open the doorway between these two cells, then we can help the artists copy the paintings."

"Go ahead," Goper said. "I'm listening."

"If we get the paintings copied quickly for you," Travis said, "then Ms. Günerro will see your power, your attitude, your leadership, and she will be forced to make you head of Good Company Security."

"That's a good idea!" Ekki said.

"You're right," Goper said, standing. "That's a fantastic idea."

"It was your idea, Goper," said Travis.

"Get the keys," Astrid said.

"Wait! I'll give the order here," Goper said. "Ekki, get the keys."

"Wait, wait, wait," Travis said. "You have to bring the stolen paintings into our rooms so we can copy them."

"I know that!" Goper said. "Ekki, get the keys *and* the paintings. Now!"

"Need some fans too," Alister said. "A lot of paint smells, you know."

"I'm not stupid," Goper said as he marched off. "I'm nearly head of security."

By midmorning the door between the two cells was open, and the artist monks had toted the stolen paintings into their side of the dungeon.

Goper and Ekki took up their positions on the plastic chairs out in the hallway while the New Resistance kids helped the monks.

With the fans whirring at top speed, the Burmese boys began copying the artwork.

Nalini gathered the New Resistance kids.

"This is great that we have the paintings," she whispered. "But we have to get them *and* ourselves out of here, and having Alister pick the locks is not going to get us very far."

"Maybe Hervé will show up again," Astrid said.

"Don't hold your breath," Kerala said.

"Lucas is alive," Jackknife said, "and he'll be here in a little while."

"You think?" Alister asked.

"He's our friend," Jackknife said. "And you can count on him."

CHAPTER 37

CAFÉ CON LECHE

Lucas's eyes sprang wide open.

For a second he didn't know where he was. He lay still and let his mind fill with data and ideas. He replayed the previous day hour by hour. An art heist at the Reina Sofía. A scary train ride.

And now he was in a cottage in a vineyard in Andalusia in southern Spain. As his brain fully booted up, he figured it was 8:37 in the morning. Five hours of sleep would have to do.

The whole place smelled of freshly boiled eggs and coffee. Sunlight came through a dirty glass window.

Across the room the old man was talking on a telephone that was attached to the wall, a long curly cord connecting it to the receiver. Lucas listened, but he couldn't quite understand what the man was saying. A minute later he hung up.

"Buenos días," the old man said.

"Good morning," Lucas said back in Spanish.

"Do you want coffee?"

Lucas had never had coffee before. He had always considered himself a hot-chocolate man. He could ask for a *chocolate caliente*, but Lucas figured that since he was a guest and the man was being so nice he should bend a little and maybe try something new.

"Yes," Lucas said. "I would like some coffee."

The man poured black coffee in a round bowl and added lots of sugar and milk.

"Café con leche," he said, putting the coffee with milk on the table.

The drink was delicious. Lucas sat on a stool and devoured his bread-and-butter breakfast.

After a few minutes the caffeine in the coffee kicked in, and Lucas felt like he was ready to rocket to the moon.

"Wow!" he said, his eyes nearly popping out of his head. "No wonder people like this," he said in English.

The old man smiled at the boy.

Once the coffee had coursed through his veins, Lucas calmed down a bit and began to lay out his day.

"I have to get to Granada today," Lucas said in Spanish. "Is there any possible way you could give me a lift?"

"I don't have a car or truck on the farm," the man said, "but I have horses. Do you ride?"

"I trained at a dude ranch in Montana two summers ago."

"English or Western?"

"Both," Lucas said. "My father insists that we prepare for anything that might come our way."

"Your father is a smart man."

Lucas and his host went into the barn. The old man paced back and forth in front of the stalls, carefully choosing the right horse. He stopped and put his boot on one of the gates.

"I know who you are," he said.

Lucas gulped. "You do?"

"You work with a group called the New Resistance—isn't that right?"

"Yes," Lucas said, hoping this wasn't a bad thing.

"I spoke with a friend on the phone this morning," the man said. "Her name is Aleta, and she flies for the Spanish Civil Guard. All the farmers out here know her and her grandson."

Lucas didn't quite understand why this man was telling him this.

"Aleta lives on the grounds at the Alhambra, and she told me this morning that your friends were taken to the Good Art Institute of Granada, which is located at the Alhambra."

"That's a good thing," Lucas said.

"Depends," said the old man. "Aleta tells me that it's also an old torture chamber that is in the basement of the hotel there."

"What about the paintings?"

"A Van Gogh Art Movers truck pulled into the hotel just before sunrise this morning. The stolen paintings are presumably there with your friends."

"Did she call the police?"

"Yes," said the man. "They came and found nothing."

"But does your friend think they're still there?"

"Yes," he said. "No question."

CHAPTER THIRTY-SEVEN

"How do I get in?"

"You want to break into a torture chamber?"

"I want to help my friends," Lucas said. "And find the stolen paintings."

"Very well," said the old man. "Aleta tells me the New Resistance is very strong. I trust her."

"We try."

"This may help you then," explained the old man. "The hotel is made of stone and it is very old. On the south side, underneath the trees, a portion of the original construction built by the Arabs in the thirteenth century is now aboveground. You might find an opening there."

The man took some horse-riding clothes from a peg on the wall and handed them to Lucas.

"These belonged to my son many years ago," he said. "You are about the same size."

While Lucas changed into the clothes, the old man saddled up a beautiful black Andalusian stallion.

Now wearing a *campera* jacket, *caireles* pants, and a Cordoba hat, Lucas looked like an authentic Spanish cowboy.

"Vaquero," the man said, handing Lucas the reins.

Lucas loved being called a cowboy in Spanish. He fixed himself in the saddle and patted the horse on the neck.

"What's his name?" Lucas asked.

"Amigo."

"I'm sorry but I don't know your name," Lucas said.

"Romero."

The old man handed Lucas a hand-drawn map. Lucas glanced at it and memorized it.

"There is food in the saddlebag," Romero said.

"Thanks," Lucas said. "What do I do with Amigo when I get to the Alhambra?"

"Leave the horse with Aleta," he said. "She, too, is your friend."

Lucas clucked and said giddyup in Spanish, *"¡Arre!"*

The horse turned and walked out of the barn. They cantered through the vineyard and down a dirt road and into the Spanish countryside.

Amigo and Lucas traveled all day past almond plantations, sunflower fields, and *pueblos blancos*—small, whitewashed villages that reflected the sun.

Around three in the afternoon, Lucas stopped at a creek to water Amigo. He found dried sausage and bottled water for himself in the saddlebag. Under a shade tree the horse and the boy took a nap, a true Spanish siesta. When the heat seemed less, Lucas hopped back on Amigo, and they rode well past sunset until they arrived at the Alhambra.

The horse's hooves clomped up the stone walkway. At the back gate Lucas slid out of the saddle and rang the bell. Soon a woman with long hair appeared.

"Buenas noches," she said in a whisper. "Good evening. I'm Aleta. We've been expecting you."

NO PLAN

The next morning Lucas opened his eyes, and again for a moment he wondered where he was. He had slept in so many different places that he was almost getting used to it.

He was in a small bed in what appeared to be a shed. Old gardening tools and machine parts were scattered around the room. In the corner were a sink and toilet. Horse tack hung from wooden pegs, and blankets were stacked in piles on the floor.

Above him a spider spun a web in the rafters. Lucas watched her spinning her lines back and forth. Near the center of the web a dead hornet curled in a tight ball. He hoped it wasn't an omen.

Lucas heard the blades of a helicopter outside. He glanced out the window toward the noise and spotted Amigo in the corral where he had left the stallion the night before. Just beyond the fence he could see the helicopter's tail rotor twirling.

It was time. Lucas swung his bare feet onto the dirt floor. Immediately his butt started killing him. Riding a horse for almost nine hours had taken its toll. He closed his eyes again and let his mind catch up with where he was.

He had arrived at Aleta's house at the Alhambra gardens. He had a lot to do, and it was already 8:56, he figured.

The door to the shed opened, and the distinct smell of ham drifted in. A stocky and muscular boy with a baby-blue headband stepped into the room. Lucas guessed he was about fourteen years old.

For a long second the kid stared at Lucas's bed-head hair.

"My name is Rafa," he said in English. "I'm Aleta's grandson."

"I'm—" Lucas started to say.

"I know who you are," Rafa said. "I met your friends last night."

"How did you meet them?"

"I clean tables in the hotel, and Ms. Günerro paid me to take food into the dungeon and serve your friends dinner."

"Are they okay?"

"They're busy."

"What do you mean? Busy?"

"They have arranged for the artists to copy the stolen artwork."

"So the paintings *are* there?"

"When I took the food," Rafa said, "one of the girls told me they were copying the paintings."

Lucas was still groggy. "Why are they helping copy the paintings?"

"The boys told me that Lucas Benes would be

coming soon and that you would have a plan to get the original paintings out."

"I'm glad they have confidence in me," Lucas said, "but to be honest, I don't have a plan."

"My grandmother and I can help."

"Where exactly are the paintings?" Lucas asked.

"Your friends and the paintings are in the hotel basement, hidden in an old dungeon behind a false wall."

"*¡El barco!*" said a woman's voice from the other room.

"The boat?" Lucas asked.

"You need to get up. It's nearly nine o'clock, and we have some other news to share with you."

CHAPTER 39

I'M POSSIBLE

In a few minutes Lucas was standing in the kitchen. Sunlight shone through a window above the sink. A giant ham was perched on a cutting board on the counter. On the breakfast table there were newspapers and a vase filled with flowers.

Aleta made both boys *café con leche*, and she put a plate of ham and day-old bread on the table. The boys sat and ate and dunked the crunchy bread into the coffee milk.

Lucas got a good look at the woman. She didn't look old like a grandmother. She was thin and wore dark pants and a leather vest over a white shirt.

"Tell him what I learned," she said to her grandson in Spanish. "Your English sounds better than mine."

"My grandmother works with the Spanish Civil Guard," Rafa said. "This morning she was flying the helicopter around the port in Gibraltar. The ship captains she works with said that two men named Creed and Chapman were at the harbor and had just bought one of Ms. Günerro's superyachts on the spot."

"Coach Creed and Rufus Chapman bought a boat!"

Aleta flipped the newspaper over to the business page.

A headline read GOOD COMPANY TRIES TO AVOID BANK-RUPTCY BY SELLING LITERALLY EVERYTHING.

"What was the name of the boat?" Rafa asked his grandmother. "The yacht?"

Aleta said, "The *Thimblerig.*"

The pieces of an idea fell together in Lucas's mind. He muttered, "So if the boys in yellow robes, the monks, are also here . . ." He paused. "Is the *Thimblerig* in the port of Gibraltar?" Lucas asked.

"Yes," Aleta said.

"What about kids?" Lucas asked. "Were there any children with Coach Creed and Rufus Chapman?"

"I didn't see any," Aleta said. "But when I refueled at the Gibraltar airport, there was a huge 747 that I had never seen before. Is this the New Resistance airliner?"

"Were there registration marks?" Lucas asked.

"Air traffic control," Aleta said, "told me the plane was called white bird one."

"Yes," Lucas said. "They're there, and that's where we're going too."

Lucas's plan gelled. "How far away is Gibraltar?"

Aleta said, *"Doscientos kilómetros."*

"Two hundred kilometers," Lucas said. "One hundred and twenty-five miles roughly. How long does that take by car?"

"In my truck," Rafa said, "it takes more than three hours to the port."

"You're a kid and you have a truck?"

"I drive when I'm working on the farms around here, like at Mr. Romero's, where you got the horse."

"By air," Aleta said, "it takes less than an hour."

Lucas closed his eyes and thought for a second.

Rafa helped his grandmother clean up from breakfast. He gathered the plates and cups and put them in the sink, where she washed and dried them.

"I have an idea," Lucas said, "that just might work."

Rafa turned off the faucet, and he and Aleta turned and stared at Lucas.

"One thing I've learned," Lucas said, "is that sometimes you have to think differently from everyone else. With the Good Company you have to do this all the time."

"So what's your plan?" Rafa asked.

"When I was at the Reina Sofía a few days ago, the Good Company broke out of the museum by knocking down a wall," Lucas explained. "Then Romero who gave me the horse told me that the stones on the south side of the Alhambra palace were old, like thirteenth-century old to be exact. Maybe we could do the same. We could use the Good Company's backward thinking against them and break *into* the hotel just like they broke *out of* the museum."

"That would be nearly impossible," Rafa said. "We only have gardening tools here. It would take forever."

Aleta shook her head. "When I was a child, I wanted to be a pilot. My father told me that it would be difficult for a woman to get a flying license, but he also told me this," she said. "The impossible ceases to exist the moment you go beyond the borders of possible."

Lucas thought about this.

"If you *want* to make it happen," Aleta said, "then *make* it happen."

CALL IT EVEN

The side-view mirrors of the scooter rattled in the wind.

Lucas held on to the chrome bar in the back while Rafa twisted his wrist, gassing the moped through the old town of Granada.

The boys bumped down cobblestone streets and past tiny cars parked on narrow lanes. It was still morning, and there were not many people out. Near a park with green football fields Rafa pointed at a roundabout. At first Lucas didn't quite understand what was here. Rafa nodded and Lucas knew the spot was a backup meeting point, just in case.

After a few minutes Lucas and Rafa arrived at the train station parking lot.

Before he hopped off the scooter, Lucas glanced at the mirrors again and spotted two blurs of Day-Glo yellow moving toward them.

"I'm going to need a distraction," Lucas said. "For just a few minutes."

"You're going to go straight across the tracks?"

"More or less," Lucas said. "The Good Company train is parked off to the side. But I'll have to get past those guys in yellow jackets."

"Don't worry about them," Rafa said. "I'm a teenager too, and I know how to draw attention to myself."

Lucas left Rafa in the parking lot and made his way to the train platform. It was the first time all day that he noticed he was still wearing the riding clothes Romero had given him. He still looked like a Spanish cowboy. He was about to rob a train, and the outfit gave him an extra burst of confidence.

The passengers expecting trains didn't seem to pay Lucas or his fashion any attention. He tapped his boots and surveyed the scene. He only had to wait for maybe ninety seconds.

A high-pitched whine came screaming through the station. On his scooter, Rafa rode a wheelie straight through the middle of the lobby, around the benches, and out to the back, where he skidded to a stop on the platform.

Lucas and the passengers moved out of his way. The guys in yellow jackets stopped their work and dropped their tools. With a swarm of Day-Glo chasing behind him, Rafa spun the scooter around and blasted down the platform toward a storage building.

While everyone focused on the speeding scooter, Lucas jumped down onto the track bed and sprinted across the rails. He hopped up on the next platform and climbed between rows of parked locomotives until he came to the Good Company train.

Bleach and her clique were in the café car sitting at several tables. Lucas crouched under the windows, hugging the side of the train all the way down. Heat radiated off the metal containers.

The smell hit him before he got there. Stinky armpits. Lucas dropped to tracks and crawled underneath Hircus's compartment. With little trouble he jimmied the loose sheet metal out of the way and was back in the car with the old goat.

"Hey, buddy," Lucas said, patting Hircus on the head.

"Baa."

It wasn't the time to sit and chat it up with his former roommate though. Lucas moved from this car through the train, past the compartment that used to hold the paintings, and into the tool section. He could hear the Curukian girls giggling in the café car.

Bleach and the others had nearly killed him a few days earlier. The girls were beyond brainwashed. What Lucas was planning to do that afternoon would take time, and he didn't need Curukian girls getting in the way. He would have to contain them.

Moving as quickly and as quietly as he could, Lucas grabbed two small jackhammers and scooped up a spool of extension cords.

He scurried back through the middle of the train and dropped his borrowed equipment through the hole and onto the tracks below.

Then he untied Hircus. "Just keep saying baa," he said. "Okay, buddy?"

"Baa."

Lucas tiptoed back to the café car. He wrenched opened the metal lock and stuck his head inside. Most of the girls were now behind the bar, eating candy.

"Hey, girls," he said. "That's not vegetarian. That candy is made with beef!"

"It's Lucas!" Bleach screamed. "I knew he'd come back. Get him."

The girls lunged at Lucas, but he slammed the door in their faces and rocketed through the train. Bleach and company followed. Lucas leaped into Hircus's stinky train compartment. He left the door slightly ajar and then slipped down through the slot in the floor. He twisted the piece of metal back into place, blocking the opening.

From above his head he could hear Hircus braying, "Baa, baa."

Bleach yelled, "Turn on the light."

Lucas crawled under the train. Above him he heard the other Curukian girls speak for the first time.

"Ah," one said. "What's that smell?"

"It's awful."

"There's no light in here."

"I hear Lucas in the corner," said another.

Bleach yelled. "Don't let him get out!"

Lucas climbed up between the two train cars and slammed the door to Hircus's compartment closed. He looped a padlock through the metal bar and clicked it to lock the girls inside.

"Let's call it even," Lucas muttered. "You tried to

drown me the other day, and today I'm giving you some free hot yoga classes."

With the Curukian girls banging on the door, Lucas scooped up his borrowed tools from underneath the train and headed out. Now toting the jackhammers and extension cords, Lucas circumnavigated the train station. He cut through the park with the football fields and waited for Rafa at the roundabout he'd pointed out earlier.

The scooter sounded like a chain saw buzzing up the street. In a moment Rafa came into view and skidded to a stop in the crosswalk.

Still shouldering the jackhammers, Lucas straddled the seat and held on with his legs. From there the boys rode straight to the hotel at the Alhambra.

The sun was blazing hot and the boys kept a low profile as they sneaked under a canopy of trees. They made their way to the south side of the hotel. On the far corner, just like Romero had said, was an ancient wall that looked like it was ready to crumble.

"Perfect," Lucas said.

Rafa unraveled the extension cords and strung them around the building to an outlet. By the time he got back, Lucas had borrowed a sheet of the green fencing used to protect the new trees. The boys put stakes in the ground and set up a makeshift work tent.

"This is going to make a lot of noise," Rafa said.

"We'll have to take our chances."

Now mostly hidden from the outside, they fired

up the jackhammers. The two boys worked side by side, chipping away at the concrete grout around the stones. It did make a lot of noise but it took a lot less time than Lucas had imagined. As soon as there was space around one of the rocks, Lucas decided to give it a nudge.

Both boys pushed the boulder with their feet, and to their surprise the stone clunked down into the room.

Thud.

The hole was about as big as a pet door. With his head upside down Lucas peered through the opening in the wall.

"I hope you're breaking us out," Travis said.

"Something like that," Lucas said.

Lucas knew he had to do more than just get his friends out. He had to get the paintings, too. But at that moment, he had run out of ideas.

ART EXCHANGE

Lucas knelt and looked through the hole he had just created in the stone wall.

Jackknife looked up from the opening. "Who's that with you?" he asked.

"This is Rafa," Lucas said, gesturing behind him. "He's my new friend, and he says that you're making copies of those paintings?"

"That's true," Travis said. "Mostly it's *our* new friends, these monks, who painted them."

New friends? Lucas thought for a second. *Friends really are the most important things in life.*

The smell of paint and chemicals blasted Lucas in the face.

"Is that why it stinks in there?" Lucas said.

"We've been busy painting, mate," Alister said. "We've got linseed oil, turpentine, acrylics, watercolors. You name it."

Jackknife waved a brush. "You want me to paint your picture?"

Nalini punched him. "No kidding right now."

"We've got to get out of here," Astrid said.

Rafa moved closer to the opening and spoke to everyone on the inside. "It won't take us that long to make a hole big enough for you to get out of, but it might take us a little while to cut a hole big enough to get the paintings out."

"I'm not sure it's the best idea," Astrid said, "for us to take the paintings with us. At least not right now."

"We can't leave them here for Ms. Günerro," Nalini said. "She'll either sell them or, worse, destroy the originals."

"True," Lucas said. "I think we can do both."

"How do you propose to do that?" Astrid said.

"Well," Lucas said. "Coach Creed and Rufus bought the *Thimblerig*."

"What!" said the kids down in the cell.

"It's moored in the harbor at Gibraltar," Rafa said.

"If we can get you all and the paintings out," Lucas said, "Rafa has a truck to take us to Gibraltar where the other New Resistance kids are."

"How do you know the others are there?" Astrid asked.

"Rafa's grandmother spotted White Bird One at the Gibraltar airport."

"Let's get crackin', mates," Alister said.

Still looking through the small hole in the wall, Lucas asked, "What about Ms. Günerro and Goper and Ekki? Where are they?"

Travis said, "They just came into the cell to see what the noise was."

"What did you tell them?" Lucas said.

Alister held up a mangled paintbrush. "It was this,"

he said, then jammed the brush into one of the fans, and the noise rattled like a mini machine gun.

"Whatever," Lucas said. "Are they still here?"

"They just left," Astrid said. "Travis made it seem like it was Goper's idea to start copying the paintings early so Ms. Günerro would make him head of security."

"Copying the paintings!" Lucas said. "That's a great idea!"

Jackknife added, "Ekki said they were going to the Generalife Palace for a ceremony and then to lunch."

"What time is lunch?" Lucas asked Rafa.

"In Spain," he said, "it's normally from two to four o'clock in the afternoon."

Lucas said, "So we have time."

Kerala said, "But I heard Ms. Günerro say they were going to send Bleach and her girls here to stand guard."

"Uh-oh," Lucas said.

"What?" Nalini asked.

"Nothing," Lucas said. "Are the copies of the paintings ready to go?"

Travis said, "For the most part, yes."

"I still think," Astrid said, "that it's better if we first get ourselves out safely, and then we can worry about the paintings later."

"*I* still think we can do both," Lucas said. "Would you guys do me a favor first?"

"What's that?" Nalini asked.

"Can you move all the paintings closer to this wall?" Lucas asked.

"What for?" Astrid asked.

"Just put the originals on one side and block the view of this hole in the wall with the copied paintings. Okay?"

"We got it," Alister said.

"I'll help," Nalini said. "We'll put the copies on the easels."

"Also put one in front of the window in the door," Lucas said. "So Goper, Ekki, and Ms. Günerro can't see inside."

"You keep working the jackhammer," Rafa said. "And I'll go and bring my truck."

"Great," Lucas said.

Rafa took off running through the Alhambra gardens toward his grandmother's house.

"Alister?" Lucas asked. "If Ms. Günerro and her people come back early, do you think you could do something to the door to make it so they can't look in through that keyhole?"

"Piece of cake," Alister said, securing the door with the two barrel bolts. "I can pick locks, and I can mess them up too."

"Pass me one of those jackhammers," Jackknife said. "I'll work from this side."

Lucas slipped the other jackhammer and extension cord down through the opening. The two boys set up on opposite sides of the wall and began blasting the grout, chipping away at the opening stone by stone.

In a short while Rafa came rumbling up in his truck. It was so much more than a farm truck. To Lucas it looked like an army transport truck with a navy blue tarp covering the bed.

Perfect, he thought. *Big enough for the paintings and my friends.*

Lucas and Jackknife stopped jackhammering for a second. The constant shaking was turning Lucas's arms to noodles. His whole body felt numb.

With the jackhammers turned off the gardens returned to quiet. Fortunately it was near lunchtime in Spain and no one was around. A warm wind blew through the trees, and flocks of birds flew overhead. From a distant highway the hum of tires buzzed through the air.

The kids on the inside wedged and scraped a few stones out of the way, which made the hole now big enough for them to get through.

Astrid and Travis climbed out first.

Rafa took the jackhammer from Lucas, and Kerala traded spots with Jackknife. From the outside and the inside Rafa and Kerala splintered rocks and concrete until they had created a gap in the wall large enough for the biggest painting.

"Anyone at the door?" Lucas asked.

Alister peeked through the window in the door. "No one here."

Travis and Astrid positioned themselves at the opening.

"Let's do this," Travis said. "Pass those original paintings up."

Kerala, Nalini, Alister, and Jackknife slipped *Woman and Bird at Night* up through the opening to Travis and Astrid. They handed the painting to Rafa and Lucas, who were in the bed of the truck.

The Persistence of Memory came next, followed by *Procession of Death*.

Alister called out from the cell. "Here comes the big daddy of them all."

Alister and a handful of monks carried *Guernica* on their heads. They positioned the famous painting at the opening. Just as they were about to slide it through, they heard a noise coming from the other side of the dungeon door.

Boom, boom.

Someone slapped the handle.

"Open this door!" Goper yelled. "I'm the head of Good Company Security. There's a painting blocking my view, and I can see there's something jammed in this lock. Open up!"

Someone kicked the door.

Nalini, Kerala, and Jackknife moved fast. They helped Alister and the monks hoist *Guernica* through the opening in the wall. Like a giant stretcher the painting slipped through the gap. On the outside Astrid and Travis grabbed it and passed it up to Lucas and Rafa in the truck.

The New Resistance kids on the inside scurried out of the cell and climbed onto the truck bed.

Someone continued beating on the outside of the wooden cell door.

In the back of the truck Lucas looked at the others. "What about the monks?" he asked.

"We asked them earlier to escape with us," Travis said.

Astrid said, "They're afraid of Ms. Günerro and Ching Ching."

"Doesn't seem right," Lucas said, "to just leave them behind."

Lucas stood up and looked toward Rafa. It was then that he spotted Bleach and two Curukian girls rounding the corner of the hotel.

"Time to go," Rafa said as he hopped into the driver's seat and slammed the door.

ROAD TRIP

Rafa was a surprisingly good driver for a young teen-ager. With the New Resistance kids and the stolen paintings in the bed of his truck, he sped away from the Alhambra hotel. He cut through town and headed toward the freeway. He looped the army van around a cloverleaf intersection and shifted the engine into high gear as he merged onto the national highway.

The tarp covering the bed of the truck began to flap in the breeze. The air steamed with heat and humid-ity, but swirls of wind cooled things off a little. Lucas sweated profusely, in part from the temperature but more from the rush of anxiety blazing through his veins. All the kids seemed to be in shock and didn't talk for the first few minutes.

Nalini passed around bottles of water, which they each emptied in a single gulp.

The converted army van picked up speed and cruised down the roadway to Gibraltar. Rafa seemed confident. The knobby tires on the truck thumped across the ridges in the pavement, faster and faster, until the kids looked like they might fall asleep. They probably could have napped the whole way had it not been for Jackknife.

The Brazilian kid wasn't close to being tired. He was the opposite. Fired up. He spread open the slit in the canvas, leaned out over the gate, and screamed as loud as he could. "We did it!" he yelled.

Jackknife turned around and held on to the bars on the ceiling.

"That was absolutely the best," he said. "We just stole stolen paintings. Unbelievable! Who does that?"

The others kids looked at him. Nalini yawned, and Astrid covered her face.

"We do," Jackknife said. "We just did that! From the Good Company!"

He stepped around the paintings and gave everyone high fives.

For the most part the kids seemed pretty excited about their work and what they had just accomplished.

It was fair to say that everyone was happy.

Except Lucas.

As the others were talking and laughing about how they had fooled Goper and Ekki and Ms. Günerro, Lucas sat at the far end of the bench and worried. He felt like he had forgotten something—it was the same feeling he had every time he left on a trip. That sense that he had left something behind.

Lucas zoned out as he stared at the priceless paintings in front of him. The images in the *Guernica* painting bothered him. They were people, families that had been bombed, killed, just so that Hitler and Franco could test explosives.

CHAPTER FORTY-TWO

Lucas knew it was more than that.

Franco had partly chosen the town of Guernica because his enemies had been there, but he also chose the little farming community because no one cared about it. They were people who Franco and Hitler figured just weren't good enough to worry about.

As the tarp roof flapped in the wind, Lucas consciously replayed the day's film in his head. Frame by frame. The truck. The paintings. The jackhammers. He clicked through the pictures in reverse order looking for something. Looking for what he had forgotten.

Then in his mind he heard Goper banging on the door.

Lucas looked at his friends sitting around him.

Priceless, he thought again. *A thing can be priceless. If something is more valuable than a thing, then maybe it's not a thing.*

On the other side, squished between Nalini and Kerala, he noticed some*thing* missing.

"Where's your bow tie?" Lucas asked Alister.

"You asked me to block the keyhole," Alister said. "And I was tired of that tie anyway."

The wide tires on the truck hummed, and the sound lulled Lucas back to the movie in his head. Still there was something. He dug deep into his memory and clawed his way through old scars. There was an answer he was looking for somewhere here in his mind.

Images bombarded his brain rapid fire. Lucas tried to make sense of it. He saw Gini the baby, Ms. Güner- ro and her kidnapping company, and her stolen diamonds and artwork. He cringed at the idea of a busload of kids nearly drowning in the River Seine in Paris. The scooter in Rome. Lucas shivered as he remembered being thrown off a ship and into the sea. There was Hervé and his cane. Where was he? Bleach and her clique scuba diving. He saw the shipping container at the bottom of the Mediterranean. The message from his mother spray-painted in his mind.

There are treasures far more valuable than priceless.

He looked at his friends and again at the *Guernica* painting in front of him.

Priceless painting, he thought. *A thing can be priceless. If something is more valuable than a thing, then maybe it's not a thing.*

Finally Lucas knew the answer. Knew it. In his heart and in his mind. In his DNA. Lucas sprang to his feet. He banged on the window between the back of the truck and the cab up front.

"Stop!" Lucas yelled.

He smashed his fist again on the window.

Holding the steering wheel with one hand, Rafa glanced back.

"Stop the truck now," Lucas said.

"What's going on?" Astrid asked.

The engine shook as it slowed. Rafa skidded the truck into a gravel parking lot just to the side of the road.

Lucas said, "I know what's more valuable than priceless."

SUPER PUMA

Lucas's body acted on its own.

He marched straight past the paintings and his friends and stepped through the slit in the canvas. He hopped down to the gravel parking lot and looked around.

Cars were speeding by on the highway, and the Spanish sun seemed to be baking everything. It was well over forty degrees Celsius, more than a hundred Fahrenheit.

"I'm going back," Lucas said. "You guys keep going to Gibraltar and deliver the paintings, and I'll meet you there before sunset."

"What?" Astrid asked.

Lucas didn't answer. When you know what you're doing is right, you don't have to explain it to anyone. He turned and started walking down the side of the road, all by himself, knowing in his heart what he was doing was best.

At the outset he walked quickly but soon slowed as the heat evaporated his energy. After a few moments he began to feel odd. He thought it might be the sun. Then he sensed that someone was watching him. He looked out onto the roadway to see if the Good

CHAPTER FORTY-THREE

Company bus was watching and listening.

He turned around and saw Astrid and Jackknife running to catch up with him.

"What are you doing?" he said.

"We're coming with you," Astrid said.

"You don't have to."

"We know we don't have to," Astrid said.

"You're going to need us, anyway," Jackknife said.

"We know exactly why you're going back," Astrid said.

The threesome turned and started walking.

After a few minutes in silence, Jackknife spoke. "How long is this hike going to take?" he asked.

"About an hour," Lucas said.

"We should get in some shade," Astrid said. "It's dangerously hot out here."

"Maybe we should run," Jackknife said. "And get out of the heat faster."

They turned onto Andalucía Avenue and took to the sidewalk, where the acacia trees offered a little shade. Jackknife picked up the pace and started jogging at a good clip.

A while later, they arrived back at the scene of the crime. Across the gardens Lucas spotted groups of tourists climbing a flight of stairs.

There were boot prints in the dirt around the opening they'd created, and it appeared that someone had tried to enter the dungeon. Lucas figured it was Ekki and Goper. But as far as he could tell, there were no guards or Curukians around at that moment.

Lucas peered into the room. Inside he could see that a painting still blocked the view, the barrel bolts still secured the door from the inside, and Alister's bow tie still jammed the keyhole.

Against the walls the copied paintings sat on the easels where Nalini had placed them.

"Hey," Lucas said down into the cell. "Anyone in there?"

A monk stuck his head out. "Yes?"

"It's time to go," Lucas said.

"We cannot," said the boy.

"I get it," Lucas said. "The Good Company killed my mother, and I know you're worried about your families. But no matter what, Ching Ching will think you sabotaged this heist. If you come with us, then the New Resistance can help you *and* your families."

Lucas stood up straight. "I'll get us a ride," he said to Jackknife and Astrid. "You guys get the monks out."

"They just said no," Jackknife said. "Again."

"What if they keep refusing?" Astrid asked.

"They'll have to go," Lucas said, "I'm about to make that dungeon unfit to live in."

While Astrid and Jackknife slipped through the opening and back into the cell they had escaped from, Lucas sprinted across the grounds to Aleta's house.

Twelve minutes later Lucas came back to the gap in the wall, and Astrid and Jackknife were helping the last two boys out. The others boys were huddled together under a tree, and Lucas approached them.

"I know you're scared," he said. "We all are. But if we do this right, the Good Company nightmare will be over. For good."

"Thanks for coming back," said the monk in front. "We'll help."

A wind began to blow, and a rumbling sound shook everything around them. The leaves in the trees quivered, and cones of dust swirled upward.

"Did you get us a ride?" Astrid asked.

Lucas pointed into the sky.

A Eurocopter EC225 Super Puma thundered into view.

"Yes," Jackknife said. "That's our ride?"

A fine-powder cloud erupted as the transport helicopter spun its way down to the hotel courtyard and landed.

Lucas, Astrid, Jackknife, and the monks turned to shield their eyes from the billowing dust storm.

Over the near-deafening roar of the spinning blades, Lucas called out to his friends. "Jackknife," he said. "Get the monks on board. And then run inside and hit the fire alarm."

"What?"

"Just do it," Lucas said. "Tell Aleta, the pilot, to wait for us. We'll be right back."

Jackknife took off.

"Astrid," Lucas said. "Come with me."

"Where?"

"Back inside."

CHAPTER 44

THE BEST THINGS IN LIFE

Lucas and Astrid slipped through the jackhammered hole in the wall and into the cell. Outside the main door they could hear voices.

Lucas took charge and looked at his sister. "Get something and smash all the lightbulbs in this dungeon," he said.

Astrid's eyebrows wrinkled for a second.

"Don't ask," Lucas said. "Do it."

Astrid turned and moved quickly. She went into the other cell, where the monk painters had been. There she took one of the easels and swung it into the lightbulbs, smashing them one by one.

"Hey," Goper said from the other side of the door. "What's going on in there?"

He beat on the door.

While Astrid killed the lights, Lucas snatched up the bottles of turpentine and linseed oil and then doused the easels holding the fake paintings with the flammable liquids.

Goper kicked the door. "Open up."

"Yeah," Ekki yelled. "We can't fit through that kid-sized hole you cut in the wall."

From the other room Lucas could hear Astrid

smashing more lightbulbs. Soon they were in the dark, and the only remaining light came from the opening in the stone wall.

Lucas unlocked the two barrel bolts on the wooden door. From the keyhole he gently wiggled out the bow tie and draped it around his neck.

Then he waited.

A few seconds later, Jackknife pulled the fire alarm, and the siren screamed throughout the hotel.

"Goper," Lucas yelled. "Now try your key."

When Goper opened the door, he pushed a copied painting out of his way and stepped into the room.

"Hey, Goper," Lucas said. "Congratulations on becoming head of Good Company Security."

"Um," Goper said. "Thanks?"

Ms. Günerro and Ekki hurried into the room.

"Turn on the light," Ms. Günerro said.

Ekki flicked the switch.

"It doesn't work," he said, flipping it back and forth.

"Maybe the fire alarm tripped the light switch," Goper said. "Or maybe Lucas had something to do with that."

"It doesn't matter," Ms. Günerro said, stepping forward. "What matters at this point is why Lucas Benes decided to come into this . . . this artists' studio." She glared at Lucas. "Please do tell."

Ekki and Goper stood behind their boss, nodding at every word she uttered.

"I came here," Lucas said, "mostly because I wanted to see these priceless paintings in person."

"Isn't that lovely?" Ms. Günerro said. "Lucas Benes is now an art historian."

"Sure," Lucas said. "I'm a Renaissance man."

"If you knew anything, young man," Ms. Günerro said, "you'd notice that some of those paintings behind you are originals while others are copies."

"It's so dark in here," Astrid said. "We can't really see anything."

"Goper," Ms. Günerro said. "You're head of security now. Fix the lights and do something about that awful fire alarm while you're at it. I can't even think. It's almost as bad as listening to these children."

Goper stepped out of the room.

"Soon, you'll see," Ms. Günerro said, "that the best things in life are free."

"These were not free paintings," Astrid said. "You stole them."

The muscles in Lucas's jaw clenched. He knew what he was about to do was dangerous. Very.

"You're right, Ms. Günerro," Lucas said. "At least partly right. The best things in life might be free, so long as you're free. But if you're kidnapping children, taking them away from their families and their homes, then they have no freedom at all. And that's all anyone wants anyway—to be free."

"What?" Ms. Günerro asked. "Are you some sort of philosopher-poet?"

CHAPTER FORTY-FOUR

"Yes, he is a poet," Astrid said. "And he didn't even know it."

"I agree," Lucas said, "that some great things in life don't cost any money. Some are even priceless."

"Like my new paintings," Ms. Günerro said. "They are arguably now the most valuable things on the planet."

"That's where you're all wrong," Lucas said. "The only thing more valuable than priceless is . . . people. Human beings matter more than things. Period. That's why I came back. To get the people, not the paintings."

"We have an agreement then," Ms. Günerro said. "I'll take valuables over people any day."

"But you don't have any money anymore," Astrid said. "You're broke. And your so-called Good Company is bankrupt. In fact our dad's company just bought one of your superyachts." Astrid didn't stop. "What's sad is that you're a grown-up," she said. "How could you have done all this? For all the money in the world?"

"I have trouble connecting with children," Ms. Günerro said. "I find your voices and your actions . . . well . . . childlike. I'll explain it to you this way. It's simple. I will save my company by selling copies of these priceless paintings."

"We still can't see them," Astrid said. "You don't even know how good these copies are."

"I'll show you, young lady," said Ms. Günerro. Then she yelled out the door. "Goper! Get the lights." Ms.

Günerro turned and stepped out of the room, her hand still holding the door slightly ajar.

A tiny window of opportunity had just opened.

"Ekki," Lucas whispered. "Be the hero! You've got a pack of matches on you."

"How did you know?"

"You had them on the train," Lucas said. "In Hircus's compartment."

"That's right!" Ekki said. "Good thinking, Lucas! You know, you're actually really a nice guy."

"Thanks," Lucas said. "Toss me the matches."

Ekki jammed his hand into his pocket and pulled out a little cardboard box. He shook it and flung it up in the air.

The matchbox twirled as it floated across the room. It seemed to take forever. Lucas reached up and snatched it, and the wooden sticks rattled in the cardboard.

Lucas struck a match. His face lit up for a second. From his shoulder he slid Alister's bow tie and put it in the flame. The tie must have been doused in turpentine, for the fire quickly engulfed the material.

Lucas dropped the tie to the floor, and the flammable liquids lit up like a river ablaze. The flames snaked across the concrete and hit the easels holding the fake paintings.

Within seconds the whole room lit up.

Ms. Günerro turned back into the room. Her eyes looked like they might pop out of her head.

Goper and Ekki ripped off their jackets and raced to the blaze. They slapped at the flames, trying to smother the growing inferno.

"My paintings!" Ms. Günerro shrieked. "My priceless paintings!"

Then she turned and headed out the door.

In the commotion Lucas and Astrid bolted behind the burning easels. They cut through the smoke and quickly clawed their way out of the hole in the wall. Jackknife was there and helped pull them through.

To the left the helicopter idled, and dust swirled around them. As soon as they stood up, Lucas and Astrid saw Bleach and her clique scattered across the grounds, moaning in pain.

Lucas and Astrid looked at Jackknife.

"Hervé told us this," Jackknife said. "Smoke freezes their minds, but they were in like a half trance, and they still tried to fight."

Astrid pointed at the girls on the ground. "You fought a dozen Curukians?" Astrid asked. "By yourself?"

"All you need to know," Jackknife said, "is that when they have to, monks know how to box!"

Astrid, Jackknife, and Lucas climbed aboard with the monks, and the helicopter took off.

THE ROCK OF GIBRALTAR

Aleta piloted the helicopter and transported Lucas, Astrid, Jackknife, and the monks out over the gardens of the Alhambra. Along the highway a line of fire trucks and police cars raced toward the fire, the sirens flashing.

Aleta flew over the land and the sea and toward the Costa del Sol, where the superrich play at some of the glitziest resorts in the world. The helicopter buzzed over the famous cities of Málaga and Marbella. Within about an hour they circled the Rock of Gibraltar.

Gibraltar is a British Overseas Territory located at the southern tip of Spain. It was named the Rock of Gibraltar for its massive limestone peninsula that juts out from the mainland of Europe and into the Alboran Sea that lies between Iberia and Africa.

Lucas could see the huge rock dominating the end of the continent. It was over four hundred meters, some thirteen hundred feet, high. The Eurocopter circled the eastern face of the Rock and banked a wide turn into the harbor at Gibraltar.

Sitting in the middle of all the other boats was the Globe Hotel's first superyacht. The whole New Resistance team covered the deck of the *Thimblerig*. The kids were jumping up and down and waving, going crazy. Lucas spotted Hervé waving his cane and Rufus tipping his top hat. Mike and his crew of Indonesians were there too.

Aleta lowered the helicopter into position. When they were about ten meters, roughly thirty-three feet, from the water, she spoke into her headset. "This is as close as I can safely get."

Jackknife flung open the side door. He turned around, balanced his shoes on the edge, and did a backflip straight into the harbor.

The monks didn't hesitate either. They sprang from their seats and leaped out the door like kids at a summer-camp lake.

When the last monk plunged into water, Jackknife was already climbing up the ladder and onto the deck of the superyacht.

Lucas and Astrid waved good-bye to Aleta.

They held hands and jumped from the helicopter and splashed into the sea.

CHAPTER 46

EPILOGUE

That night the chef on board the superyacht cooked crab legs, and the kids ate until they were stuffed. After dinner, Nalini took Gini to bed, and Lucas, Astrid, and friends gathered together in front of the giant TV.

Three beeps came across the television and all the kids in the room looked up.

A man and a woman sat at an anchor desk and began to report the news. Across the bottom of the screen a red line flashed: BREAKING NEWS: STOLEN SPANISH PAINTINGS RETURNED.

The news anchor spoke. "Picasso's *Guernica*, stolen from the Reina Sofía Museum in Madrid two days ago, has mysteriously appeared at police headquarters in the British Overseas Territory of Gibraltar located at the southern tip of the Iberian Peninsula.

"The artwork has now been transferred to Spanish authorities. The Picasso painting as well as the others stolen during the brazen heist are on their way back to their home."

Another red line flashed across the screen: BREAKING NEWS: UNICEF REPORTS RECORD NUMBER OF MISSING CHILDREN FOUND.

CHAPTER FORTY-SIX

The anchorwoman spun in her chair and faced another camera.

"The United Nations Children's Fund, UNICEF, was overwhelmed today as thousands of children who had been reported lost or kidnapped showed up at local UNICEF offices worldwide.

"UNICEF is headquartered in New York City and provides long-term humanitarian assistance to children and mothers and their families worldwide.

"From Cincinnati to Jakarta to Helsinki, officials say they were stunned today by a number of missing children turning up. The head of UNICEF said the reason for the surprise influx came from an anonymous tip in the Barcelona office last week, and since then their offices have been overrun with children who are now being returned to their families."

Lucas looked over at Hervé. He was beaming.

Another red line flashed across the screen: BREAKING NEWS: GOOD COMPANY BROKE.

"For today's business news," said the anchor, looking straight ahead, "the multinational megacompany known as the Good Company is officially gone.

"The company filed for bankruptcy, and a spokesperson said today, quote, "we have no money left," End quote. The Good Company leaves owing billions of dollars to hundreds of countries, companies, and people across the globe.

"A group called Out of Africa, led by Mr. Lu Bunguu, has bought the Good Company weapons division, aptly named the Good Guns Company.

"The Good Chemical Division has been sold to Ching Ching Enterprises for an undisclosed amount.

"It's also rumored that the Globe Hotel, a world-wide chain of boutique spas and resorts, has made a bid to take over the entire Good Company hotel chain.

"Company head Ms. Siba Günerro has reportedly resigned; however, her whereabouts are unknown. The CEO was last seen at a hotel that was on fire at the Alhambra in Granada, Spain.

"There were no injuries, and the building was not damaged. Firefighters said that someone had unmistakably tripped the fire alarm *before* the blaze actually started. Interestingly, the only thing destroyed in the fire were *copies* of the paintings stolen from the Reina Sofía Museum.

"Police now believe that Ms. Günerro is the prime suspect in the art heist and that she had planned to sell the copied paintings on the black market in order to help her company stop losing money."

The anchorwoman turned and faced the gentleman sitting next to her. He wore a dark suit and glasses and had gray hair.

"In today's opinion segment," said the woman, "we have Bernie Keyser from 'Wall Street Minute' to give us his take on today's big news."

The newsman picked up the next story.

"I'll be brief. In my opinion the Good Company is bad, rotten to the core. This group has had allegations of misconduct for years, and police have never been able to make any crimes stick to Ms. Günerro or her thugs, oddly known as Curukians.

"People who study worldwide crime know full well the tragedies that this one cheating company has inflicted on so many. I for one am happy, thrilled, to hear that the Good Company has finally met its match. Apparently a group of children brought down this awful organization. Maybe grown-ups should listen to children more often and treat them like adults. The world might be a better place if we did. That's just my opinion.

"In closing, I've got two things to say to this so-called Good Company.

"Good-bye and good riddance."

Mr. Benes turned the television off, and Rufus Chapman began whistling a sleepy song. Soon the kids migrated to their cabins.

Lucas went to bed that night and crawled into his bunk. For the first time in a long time he slept like a baby, knowing at that very moment everything was right with the world.

A CALL TO ACTION

Do the write thing. Write a review online!

Visit www.crimetravelers.com for information on speech & Skype requests.

If you've read this far in the series, I'd really love to hear your thoughts in an online review.
www.bit.ly/crimetravelers

CPSIA information can be obtained
at www.ICGtesting.com
Printed in the USA
BVHW080832170920
589026BV00003B/9

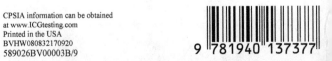